Kane's Mate

by

Hazel Gower

Includes Bonus Short Story:

Erin's Protector

Edited by Pamela Tyner

Cover Art by Live Love Media

ISBN: 978-1-937325-86-2

This book is a work of fiction and any resemblance to persons, living or dead, or places, events or locales is purely coincidental. The characters are productions of the author's imagination and used fictitiously.

Published in the United States of America by Beachwalk Press, Incorporated

www.beachwalkpress.com

Dedication

To my family for believing in me. I'm very blessed to have a wonderful husband and four beautiful children.

Acknowledgements

The most important person I want to thank is Pamela Tyner. Thank you from the bottom of my heart. I would also like to say thanks to all my writer friends, you know who you are. Thanks for the love.

Kane's Mate

Faith's life has always balanced in two worlds—the normal human world and the supernatural. Now she has to choose between the two.

Faith York is human, but she has psychic powers, which is a little odd since neither of her parents have paranormal abilities. Thankfully, the werewolf family who lived around the corner help her learn to control her powers. She instantly fell in love with the entire family, but especially Kane, the oldest son who is next in line to be Alpha. Unfortunately, Kane doesn't see Faith the same way she sees him. Heartbroken, she leaves town.

When Faith returns from two years overseas, her parents throw her a welcome home party. Faith is shocked when Kane kidnaps her from the party and mate marks her. Now she struggles with the choice of whether to leave again and live a normal life—a life she yearns for—or stay with the man she's always dreamed of and live a supernatural life.

To complicate matters further, her psychic powers intensify and she begins to have visions of an upcoming demon Armageddon. Then she learns she was switched at birth, and she has a half-brother…who is half demon.

Faith must be stronger than she ever believed possible, and maybe in the process, she can trust herself to give Kane another chance.

Content Warning: contains a sexy werewolf alpha, graphic sex, strong language, and violence

Prologue

Jamie hated that his dad made him and his brothers and sisters ride the bus home. All the other werewolves were either picked up, old enough to drive, or were too little to go to school. Today Jamie was extra eager to get home, making the forty minute bus ride seem even longer than normal. It had been a week since the four human families had moved in. Three of the families had children. His dad had told them all to be nice to the humans, because they were there to help with the mine. Jamie didn't care about that, he was just excited to have more kids around to play with so he didn't have to play with his stupid brothers, and especially his sisters. His mum had said to give them a couple of days to settle in before he bothered them, so he had given them a full week just to be safe.

Jamie knew he would have to avoid the forest around them as his dad had told the humans to keep out of the forest due to wild animals and mine holes.

Jamie had it all figured out—he was going to let the human kids get off, then he was going to backtrack so his stupid sisters didn't follow. Jamie watched the six kids—two girls and four boys—get out. Almost bouncing in his seat, Jamie turned to his brothers. "I'm going for a run."

The bus stopped and Jamie took off. One of his brothers, Griffen, yelled after him, "Don't annoy them for long."

Jamie stuck his tongue out as he ran to catch up with the human kids. He turned the corner to head up the hill. At the top of the hill, he saw the human kids down below surrounding a chubby little girl. He ran down the hill as the biggest of the boys pushed the little girl down, yelling at her that she was a freak, loser, fatty, and that nobody liked her. Tears rolled down the little girl's dirty face as she stared up at them. She didn't look old enough to be at school. She was a small girl with olive brown skin, brown eyes, and long brownish red hair that was falling out of a braid.

Just as the other kids were about to kick her, Jamie grabbed the older two. "Don't you hurt her. She's just a little girl," he screamed. "Pick on someone your own size."

The oldest boy laughed. "What about you?" he replied.

Then he tried to push Jamie, but Jamie moved out of the way and the boy fell over. The others went to attack Jamie. He looked up at them and knew his wolf shone through, because they backed up as Jamie told them, "She's only little, you should feel ashamed."

One of the boys laughed and yelled back, "She's a fat

freak!"

Jamie growled. "Go home and leave her alone."

The little girl became brave and stood up next to him and told them, "I would do what he says. His daddy is one of the owners of the mine, and if you hurt him your daddy won't have a job."

The five kids looked at Jamie, then ran home.

Jamie turned to the little girl and asked, "Are you okay?"

She nodded, staring at him curiously.

Jamie heard his oldest brother calling him, "Jamie, you okay? What happened?"

Jamie looked up at his eldest brother Kane. He had an odd look on his face as he stared at the little girl.

"Yes, Kane, I'm fine. Those kids were picking on this little girl." Jamie puffed up his chest. "And I saved her."

* * * *

Kane looked down at the wide-eyed little girl. She didn't look older than five. She was a cute little thing, even with the blotchy red eyes from crying, the dirt on her cheeks, and her hair everywhere from falling out of the braid that it was supposed to be in. His wolf inside him thought she was adorable, it wanted to rip to shreds the kids who had picked on her.

The odd reaction of his wolf caused him to stare at the girl, looking for something, anything that would make him understand why his wolf reacted that way. He knew it couldn't be magic, as wolves were supposedly immune to all magic bar their own, but maybe this little girl who looked up at him with complete trust, admiration, and love…could she be different? Why would she be looking at him that way? It was Jamie who had saved her. Kane shook his head. He must have misinterpreted something.

She smiled up at him with a top tooth missing. "Hi. Can I see you turn into a wolf?" She turned to Jamie and added, "I'm not a little girl, I'm a big girl. I go to school now and everything."

Kane couldn't help but laugh. "Yes, I can see. What's your name?"

She turned back to him, and her smile got even bigger. "I'm Faith York. Now can I see your wolf? If you won't show me, maybe Jamie will show me his." Faith turned to Jamie. "I bet you're really cute and cuddly!"

Jamie groaned, and Kane laughed harder at Jamie's tortured face.

"I won't call you a pup, cos I know how much you hate that. I wish I had brothers and sisters. You're so lucky to have twelve people in your family. I told my mum that we were surrounded by werewolves, and she said I have an overactive imagination, whatever that means, but don't worry, I won't tell anyone else because I know now that it's a secret. You save us from all the bad things," Faith said.

Kane and Jamie stared open-mouthed at Faith as she smiled up at Kane.

"You're really pretty. You can be my Prince Charming." As she grabbed Kane's hand, she gasped and seemed to go into a trance for a minute or two, her eyes becoming even bigger.

Faith grinned up at them and headed in the opposite direction to her house, dragging him with her.

Chapter 1

It's so nice to be home, Faith thought. Her parents were throwing her a welcome home party, and she couldn't wait to see her second family. She had missed Jamie and his family so much. Faith's parents had picked her up from the airport yesterday, and she'd spent a relaxing afternoon with them. But tonight she hoped everyone she loved would be there, bar one. She couldn't see him, not yet, she needed time to settle, build up her walls against him. Faith shook her head and finished getting ready for her party.

Two hours later, the party had started and Faith was chatting to all her friends, but she couldn't stay focused on the conversation around her, because she was eagerly awaiting some of the most important people in her life. Her werewolf family was late, and she was starting to get upset.

She had been away for two years with only phone contact with the Wolfens. She never missed speaking to at least one of them every night. They were the reason she had come home, and why she'd left in the first place. It's not that she wasn't grateful to them, especially as they'd helped her learn to control her psychic gifts, but they always seemed to take over and overprotect her. She sighed and gave herself a little shake, hoping it would get her back into the conversation around her.

When Faith finally felt her wolf family arrive, she smiled, excused herself from the friends she was talking to, and ran outside to greet them. Faith kissed all the werewolves, and when she reached Jamie she jumped on him, kissing his cheek. "I missed my best friend so much," Faith told him.

Jamie chuckled. "We talked almost every day."

"I missed your hugs, and I miss your stupid jokes, they don't have the same effect over the phone." Faith kissed both of his cheeks.

She looked up and saw Kane first before she felt him. He was special. Faith loved her werewolf family, but the love she had for Kane was different, more intense, sexual, a love she felt to the bottom of her soul. The problem was, he didn't want her.

Faith looked over Jamie's shoulder, trying for a casual, "Hi, Kane."

She turned her head back to Jamie before she did something stupid like jump on Kane and kiss him to show him how much she loved him and didn't want to live without him anymore.

Without thinking of the consequences, she kissed

Jamie on the mouth, trying not to put all her regret and self-hatred at loving Kane into it. Jamie seemed startled at first, but then he grabbed her arse to hold her closer to him, and he really got into it.

Faith wished she loved Jamie the way she loved Kane. God, she wished she felt something from this kiss. Nothing…she felt nothing for Jamie beyond friendship.

She sighed in thanks when her mother called her inside as she had an overseas caller. Faith walked into the house, not daring to look back at the group, knowing if she did she would have to acknowledge what was going on.

* * * *

Kane got out of his car and froze as chocolate and vanilla assaulted his senses. He looked for the source, terrified because he knew who it would be. His gaze fell on an absolutely gorgeous, grown-up Faith, and his wolf stood at attention for the first time in more than four years. It growled in his head *mate, take, mate.*

Kane stared at Faith as she greeted his family. When she came to Jamie she jumped on him, kissing his cheek. Kane fought with his wolf as he waited patiently for Faith to acknowledge him. All she did was look at him with a blank expression and say "hi" then turn her head to kiss Jamie on the mouth.

Kane snapped. He growled and lunged for Jamie only to be held back by his brothers, Rane and Arden. "Mine," he snarled as he struggled to free himself.

Kane knew he wasn't being rational. Jamie was his brother and Faith's best friend, but it seemed his wolf, and deep down he admitted to himself, *he* didn't care. The kiss ended when Faith was called inside. She excused herself and left without even looking back.

Jamie turned to him, and his face paled and his eyes widened as the realization seemed to sink in. Jamie screamed, "No, no, no, you can't have her. She can't be your true mate."

Kane surged forward again, and this time he found himself free. He got up in Jamie's face, making sure his alpha wolf showed, and bellowed, "Mine. Don't touch her again. Next time I will kill you, brother or not."

Kane knew he was overreacting, but his wolf had taken over. He followed his nose inside where he found Faith on the phone in her bedroom. She turned to him with a stunned expression as she ended her call. Kane grabbed the phone and threw it on her pillow. He picked a still shocked Faith up, threw her over his shoulder, and took her out the back to avoid being seen. Arriving at his car, he placed her in the passenger seat, telling her "don't move", and then got in and drove away.

Obviously stunned, she didn't say anything until they were on their way. "Dr. Wolfen, take me back to my party, right now," demanded Faith.

Kane knew why she wasn't calling him by his given name, by calling him Dr. Wolfen she was creating space between them and she didn't have to acknowledge how close they had once been.

Frustrated, Kane raked his hand through his hair. "Why? You're close to everyone in my family, all of them heard from you while you were overseas. My parents already treated you like a daughter. God, you used to be my constant shadow when I was home. When you were little I helped you control your gifts. What happened? You just started avoiding me, stopped talking to me. You wouldn't even be in the house when I was there." He shook his head. "That's why my wolf doesn't talk to me anymore, because over four years ago you stopped talking to me. I wondered why, when any information came up about you my wolf would perk up. I should have known, but you're so young. There's a fourteen year age difference between us. I guess that's why I never guessed."

A few minutes later, they arrived at his house. Parking his car in the driveway, Kane grabbed a stunned, opened-mouth Faith—which he felt pretty good about, as it was hard to get anything by her—and carried her inside.

He placed Faith on his bed and stared at her. She was the most beautiful thing he had ever seen. His wet dream had come to life. Faith was still short, it didn't look like she'd grown any since he last saw her, still just barely over five feet. Her brown-red hair was a little bit longer now, waist-length, and at that moment it was everywhere. He brushed some of the wild hair out of her warm, chocolate brown eyes. They were slightly tilted, giving her an exotic look, and they were currently glaring at him, flashing with anger. Faith had satin smooth, olive brown skin, a dainty little nose, a full bottom lip, and a slender neck. Her breasts were easily more than two handfuls—they were huge, round globes, about a large D cup he guessed. His gaze continued down to her flat tummy, and he frowned when he saw the blue belly ring that could just be seen as her dress was now pushed up to just above it. When did she get that? Pushing the thought aside for the moment, he continued his perusal, moving his gaze down her thick, toned thighs, perfect for holding on, and to her black stilettos.

Wow! Faith had really grown up and then some. Crap, no wonder she used to come home from school upset because the girls would pick on her, calling her Barbie and other things, they were jealous. He now knew why the boys wouldn't leave her alone. Faith was smoking hot. Kane shook his head, snapping out of his musing. She was all his now, no more excuses, no more stalling.

* * * *

Faith stared at Kane. God, it sucked. He just got better with age. He was tall—easily six and a half feet—with a dark complexion, thick curly dirty blond hair, and bright ocean blue eyes that captured and saw everything anytime she looked his way. She had avoided those eyes for four years, but right now they stared at her with frightening depth. His high cheekbones completed his perfect face. He even had a straight nose, which thanks to werewolf healing had remained straight despite being broken several times. Lucky werewolves and their advanced healing abilities. His nose did have a slight point, but with his full, lush lips it just made him look better if that was possible. Argh, so unfair. She hated werewolf genes.

How was she going to get over him? Especially when he looked better than any Greek god anyone could ever imagine.

She told herself not to look down, but a quick peek wouldn't hurt, right? Glancing at the end of the bed, she bit the inside of her cheek so she wouldn't sigh at the muscles straining beneath his shirt. Oh God, just as she'd imagined…a six-pack. He was huge but still seemed all in proportion. She told herself not to look any further down, but her eyes wouldn't listen to her. Holy shit, there was a baseball bat in his pants. She gasped and looked up into his beautiful blue eyes.

"Why?" Kane said.

"Why? What?" Faith replied. What was the question again? Arghhh, he was distracting her. She needed to get out of there before she did something stupid, or said something stupid. Kane always made her feel like a love-sick idiot.

Taking a deep breath, Faith used her most authoritative voice, the voice she used when children were not listening and she needed their attention. "Dr. Wolfen, I will say it again, take me home, or I will walk home." Faith knew she should say more, she had so much to say, but every time she spoke nothing she wanted to say came out. It pissed her off. "You have no right to take me!"

He laughed at her—he frigging laughed. "Oh, Faith, yes I do."

He started removing his clothes, ripping off his shirt and pants, revealing his lovely tanned skin, his rippling muscles, and every nook and cranny of his sculptured body.

He stood in front of Faith in all his naked glory. He looked even better than she'd imagined he would look without his clothes. She gulped and sat on her hands, because she had a sudden urge to trace every one of his tattoos, and he had quite a few—her favorite were the two flowers that led to a long, thick penis that looked painfully hard. She licked her lips.

Kane shifted to his wolf form. Light shone from him as he seemed to shrink, grow long hair, and filled out into a massive dirty blond wolf.

She muttered under her breath, knowing he would hear it. "How I hate you. You're gorgeous even in your wolf form."

Kane licked her face as he proceeded to rub his fur covered body against her until she gave in, petting and hugging him. After about fifteen minutes of this Kane turned back into a man, a very naked man in Faith's arms.

Faith screeched. "Dr. Wolfen, get off me now."

"What's the difference? It's still me, princess."

Faith smiled at him. "I like you better as a wolf."

Kane stared at her, and she watched his jaw as he ground his teeth and ran his hand over his face. Faith could tell he was getting frustrated because he wasn't getting anywhere with her. "Why?"

"Why do I like you better as a wolf?"

"No, why have you avoided me for the last four years? You stopped talking to me, and any time I did manage to get a glimpse of you, you glared at me with distrustful eyes."

Faith stared at Kane, trying to figure out how to reply. She couldn't tell him that it was because of the incident that had occurred when she was sixteen. He'd come home for the weekend and she'd caught him having sex with one of his girlfriends. Later, said girlfriend had found Faith sitting on her swing in her special place in the woods and proceeded to tell her that she would never have Kane, that she had a silly crush, and she never had a chance of becoming anything to him, because he was an alpha wolf next in line and she was only human.

Faith had been heartbroken, because she knew Kane had seen and heard her when she'd walked in on them. She was also sure he'd seen her further humiliation when the girl had ridiculed her. Faith was aware Kane knew about her crush, but he said nothing, did nothing. He didn't even check to see if she was okay. Her heart was broken, and she was angry. She'd expected better from him. Maybe she had overreacted, but she was only sixteen. He was the man she loved, and she'd hoped that someday he would see her as more than just an annoying kid. She knew that he sensed she was supposed to be something special to him, even if he didn't want to acknowledge it. She didn't seem to be able to get over her anger even though it was years later. It still hurt.

Faith knew she was being childish, but no, she wasn't going to answer him. She couldn't do this again. She was getting over him, she was over him, she had decided. She had even decided she was going to take her friend Brad up on his offer and marry him and have a normal life. She had it all figured out.

Faith looked up into his eyes. "No, no way, Kane. You are not going to do this to me. I have finally got my confidence and my life back on track. I don't love you anymore, I can't. I'm going to marry someone else. Brad's coming to Australia, and when he asks me to marry him, I'm going to act surprised, and I'm going to say yes. I'm going to move to England and have a nice *normal* life! I, Faith York, do not love you anymore. I'm no longer a silly sixteen-year-old who adores you, so you, Dr. Wolfen, are going to take me home now."

Shit! Okay, that was so the wrong thing to say. She could see in Kane's eyes the wolf had taken over. He ripped Faith's clothes off and bit her shoulder, marking her as his mate.

* * * *

Kane had never been so frustrated in his life. He was the calm one in the family, the cool, collected doctor. His wolf was jealous and angry, repeating in his head that she'd been sixteen years old back then, too young to claim. *I waited patiently. She was too young then, but now she's grown. She is mine, she is ours. Deep down you knew it too.*

He had known that she was special, but he hadn't wanted to think about it because she had been so young, and she was still young.

Kane sighed. He hadn't meant to claim her like that. He knew he had to apologize for mate marking her the way he did. Kane looked up into her face, and he really was going to apologize, but as he lifted his head the beautiful look of astonishment on her face and the bright chocolate brown eyes that held warmth that he hadn't seen in years captured him. Kane couldn't resist. He placed his mouth on hers, chocolate and vanilla assaulting his taste buds as he kissed out four years of frustration, anger, confusion, and love.

At first she didn't react, but a second or two later her soft lips responded to his and her small hands started moving up his chest then around his neck. Kane gave a mental sigh of relief. He moved his hands down to explore her body, cupping her full breasts, caressing and massaging them until Faith let out a groan against his lips. He trailed one hand slowly down her tight stomach, to the heavenly juncture between her legs.

Faith moaned his name and ran her hands down his back, scratching and rubbing. Kane left her mouth, kissing his way down her neck while his hand made slow circles around her clit. She whimpered in response. When he reached the mating mark, he licked it and kissed it before moving further down her body, licking, sucking, and nipping. She tasted so good. Reaching her breasts, he sucked one nipple into his mouth while massaging the other and giving it a light pinch, then he swapped.

"Ohhhh, ahhhh, Kane. Oh, Kane."

He was in heaven, and she was calling him Kane not Dr. Wolfen. He moved his face down to that heavenly place between her thighs. When he glanced up at her, he nearly came undone at what he saw—her eyes were hooded with desire, her hair was wild everywhere, her back arched up with nipples pointed.

Faith opened her eyes a bit more, and her voice was breathless as she asked, "What's wrong?"

He looked at the goddess laid out in front of him,

smiled up at her, and replied, "Not a thing. You are perfect," and he dived in, feasting on her pussy.

* * * *

Faith couldn't believe what was happening. She was naked and Kane had mate marked her, but she didn't care because she was lost in a sexual haze of things she'd never dared imagine, but had only dreamed of. Kane, the man she had been in love with for as long as she could remember, had mate marked her, the mere human, Faith York.

Kane's mouth was heaven and hell all at once. Faith could feel his sharp fangs nip every now and then and when he did it felt so good that she moaned his name. "Kaaaannnnee!"

Kane stopped his gentle strokes of her clit and put a thick, long finger in her pussy. That felt exquisite, especially when he sucked on her clit. He added another thick finger. "Come for me, princess. I want to see you come, I want to taste you and hear you yell my name." He added a third finger and flicked his tongue over her hard nub, that's when she came undone, screaming his name as shivers of pleasure racked up her body.

"Ohhhh, Kane. Oh, I lo... Kane."

Kane looked up at her. "My God, I have never seen anyone look as hot as you do right now. I can't wait any longer, I have to have you. I need to feel that vagina of yours squeeze the life out of me." He sucked on his fingers. "You taste like heaven too. I'll take my time next time, I promise, but I have to have you now."

Kane moved back up her body, kissing, then nipping, and giving licks to sooth the nips. He reached her breasts and sucked one into his mouth, swirling his tongue around her nipple before he moved to the other, repeating his torture as he looked into her eyes. She felt his dick at her pussy. He grabbed her arse, spreading her as he thrust in, biting her breast. Pain and pleasure shot though her like she had never felt before, and she screamed as he broke through her virgin barrier. Faith looked into his shocked eyes.

"I'm so sorry. I never thought… I mean you're so beau..." He rested his forehead against hers. "I should have known—you were so tight. Wow." Then his lips curved up into a grin, and a savage gleam came to his eyes as he said, "Mine, all mine. My untouched princess. Has the pain faded yet?" She nodded and moved her bottom around. His feral eyes got brighter and his muscles flexed and tensed as he said, "No one but me. You're mine, every lush, beautiful inch mine. Mine to cherish, mine to hold, mine to love." He started to move slowly, his eyes never leaving hers. "Say it to me. Tell me no one will ever hold you or love you like this. Tell me you're mine."

Faith had never felt anything like this in her life. The pleasure that racked her body from the tip of her toes to the top of her head was so intense she didn't know how much she could take. As she looked into his eyes the intensity in his gaze sent delicious shivers of pleasure down her spine. He repeated his commands and she answered, willing to do anything he asked, just so she could feel all this insatiable euphoria.

"Yours, always have been yours, always will be."

His muscles relaxed, and he grabbed her legs and wrapped them around his back, pushing himself further in. He picked up his pace, never letting his eyes leave hers. Faith arched her body up, meeting him thrust for thrust. His hands squeezed her arse, and one moved to stroke her clit.

Her breathing labored as she panted. "I'm going to...to...ahhh, Kane."

His pace picked up faster. Kane swooped down, kissing her in time to his thrusts, and Faith shattered into a million pieces.

Kane rested his head on her shoulder. Faith heard him mutter that she was a "fucking goddess" and then he started apologizing.

"I'm so sorry, princess. This might hurt more because

it's your first time. I'm going to lock inside you. The base of my cock will swell 'til we can't move. We'll be stuck together."

Faith moaned as Kane shouted her name and she felt the base of his penis swell to lock inside her, growing impossibly bigger. Faith felt a slight burning sensation, but other than that only immense pleasure bringing her into mini-orgasms. She felt the warmth of his release. He collapsed on top of her, their languid bodies sweaty and sated.

He carefully moved them to the side with her legs still wrapped around him. Faith fought to stay awake, especially since his huge penis was still locked inside her, but with the jet lag she was unable to keep her eyes open and she drifted into a satisfied sleep.

* * * *

Kane looked down at the sleeping woman in his arms, happier than he'd been in years. Faith was his true mate, his soul mate. Who would have thought the chubby little girl who, from the ages of five to eleven, followed him around like his shadow anytime he was home would be his mate.

Between the ages of twelve to sixteen she began to get shy and embarrassed around him. Kane had caught her a couple of times in her special place in the woods on her swing, sulking or crying because some of the girls had picked on her, or a boy she liked would ask her out and she would have a vision of him talking to his buddies about her, lying and saying he did things with her. Those ones he secretly got Jamie and Devlin involved in.

Then when she was sixteen, he came home for Halloween weekend, bringing along one of the she-wolfs he was seeing at the time. He saw Faith dressed as Rapunzel, and she was everything he ever imagined she could be and more. She was in a princess's dress that went perfect with her long hair. The costume fit like a glove, showing every curve. She was the most beautiful girl he had ever seen, and when the crown on her head sparkled from the sun to her laughing face as one of the visiting young werewolves chatted her up, he remembered growling, thinking of all the ways he could get her away from the other wolves. He imagined seducing her, stripping her, and making her want no one but him. At the thought, Kane had gotten harder than he had ever been in his life. He'd been appalled with himself for thinking of a sixteen-year-old that way and went to find his then she-wolf, terrified of the thoughts he was having of Faith, as she was way too young for him.

Now that he thought of it, after that day was when Faith stopped talking to him, started avoiding him. He thought his wolf saw her as a sister and was punishing him for thinking that way about her by not talking to him and only coming out during emergencies when he needed his supernatural strength, speed, hearing, sight, or healing abilities. Shit, he should have figured it out just from that. Faith had always made him feel good and happy, and she always smelled heavenly to him no matter what she had been doing.

Kane remembered how much fun it was to be around Faith when she was little because you never knew what would come out of her mouth. He smiled, thinking of a time when she was six and they were doing activities to help her control her gifts, and she suddenly come out with "Don't worry, Kane. You won't always be the calm, collected one. You'll become a very powerful, important alpha. You will also find your true mate. Wow, so will a lot of people, all your family. But be careful, because this will be a rocky road, especially where your brothers are concerned."

He had stared in shocked awe at what had just come out of a six-year-old's mouth.

Faith had then smiled, showing her missing front teeth. "What's a true mate?"

He had explained as best he could to a little child. "Um, it's when a mommy and daddy wolf live together.

Like being married."

She had replied saying, "Oohhh, okay. Can I be Jamie or Devlin's mate?"

He had growled at that and she had laughed as he walked her to his house for dinner.

That thought brought him back to his brother. Everyone knew Jamie had been in love with Faith for years. Devlin had always thought she was great, but had fallen hard for her when he was in Afghanistan and she wrote to him every day, often sending pictures. Fuck, now that Kane thought on it, even Griffen had fallen under her spell, saying he always tried to concentrate on her feelings because she was always bright and positive.

Shit, she hadn't been kidding, this was going to be a rocky road, and not just with his brothers.

Kane slowly untangled himself from Faith and started pacing, thinking of everything he had to do. First, he needed to call work and see if he could free up some time. He knew he'd have to ask for some favors so patients could be looked after. Then he needed to check with his parents and see what the damage was so far.

Kane found his pants on the floor, got out his mobile, and was about to call the hospital when he saw his phone flashing with twenty-one missed messages. Fuck.

Your phone message inbox is full.

Message one, at 7:05 PM: "Don't you dare fucking mate her against her will or I will find a way to kill you." Jamie. Message erased.

Message two, at 7:08 PM: "Don't you dare mate her, Kane. She hates you for Christ's sake. She hasn't spoken to you in over four years." Devlin. Message deleted.

Message three, at 7:10 PM: "What the fuck is going on? Her feelings and emotions are everywhere." Shit. Griffen. Message deleted.

Message four, at 7:15 PM: "Hi, honey, it's your mother. Just a warning, your father and I will hold off the boys for as long as we can, but by the sound and look I don't know how much longer that will be."

Frustrated, Kane pressed the *delete all* button on his phone.

Are you sure you want to delete all your messages?

He knew all the messages were from his family. He gazed at Faith lying on the bed, and his lips curved up into a grin.

Hell yes. He pressed the button and then climbed back in bed so he could hold Faith. He pulled her on top of him, and she snuggled into his body mumbling, "Just give me a minute."

Kane chuckled and put the phone to his ear as he called his work.

Chapter 2

Slowly coming awake to the sound of banging, yelling, and a long, drawn-out "fuuuucck," Faith sat up, forgetting her naked state and momentarily where she was. She looked around the room, and all the events of last night came back to her. She jumped out of bed, grabbing at the bedding to wrap it around herself.

Kane chuckled at her. "Princess, after last night there is no reason to cover up, I have seen every delicious inch of you." He licked his lips.

Faith blushed. Kane chuckled again as he got out of bed and placed one of his shirts on her, which was huge and like a baggy dress. "Come on, my princess. The cavalry is here to rescue you."

She heard more yelling. Kane growled, his teeth lengthening in an angry half-change. He grew to a height of more than nine and a half feet. His bulk muscle doubled, and longer hair grew over all his body. She sighed; she had it bad when she even found him attractive in half-change.

He growled again, and through clenched teeth, he muttered, "They're going too far."

Faith grabbed his clawed hand gently. "Just remember

they're protecting me, which is what they have done most of my life. They love me, so please be nice, I love all of them."

With that Faith let go of his hand and walked out of the room, heading to the front door which burst open as she reached the lounge room and a half-changed Griffen, Devlin, and Jamie charged in followed by an amused Rane, Arden, and Kane's parents Della and Jack. Faith blushed as three huge, half-changed wolves surrounded her.

"Did he hurt you?" Jamie asked as he gently touched her neck and back.

"I'm gonna fucking kill him. Your emotions were all over the place," Griffen growled as he pressed a kiss to her forehead.

"I don't see any bruises," Devlin added as he looked her up and down.

Kane came in on a loud growl. "I would never hurt her. Get your fucking hands off her."

Kane reached for her, and with all their hands touching her, Faith started to have a vision.

Faith was surrounded by thousands of demons and minions, destruction as far as the eye could see. She was in some huge park in the city. Humans lay dead everywhere she looked. Werewolves and other creatures were fighting demons, minions, zombies, and creatures she hadn't seen before. Faith ran fighting and saving people. She saw her friends fighting, using their paranormal skills, but it wasn't enough. Everywhere she looked people she loved and knew she would come to love were fighting. Faith had a feeling hundreds of people that were major players were missing because she hadn't found them.

She ran to the center of the park where she found Rane, Kane, Della, and Jack fighting demons. She noticed vast amounts of witches and elements with chains around them connecting them to demons, forcing them to use their powers on people. She looked up and saw the largest demon she had ever seen, at least twenty-five feet in height, come out of nowhere and give a killing blow to Jack. Faith and Della screamed as he fell to the ground. She ran forward only to be grabbed by Kane. The largest demon, which had just killed Jack, laughed, a scratchy sound.

"Come here now, Faith. I always wanted my own soothsayer, especially one as talented and beautiful as you." He laughed again. "They're so hard to find. Ah, but I've been watching you. You have so much potential. It is foretold you'll be one of the greatest if you apply yourself. Pity you wanted to be normal, but don't worry, we'll work on it, and we will make this Armageddon on your world look like child's play. The other worlds won't know what hit them. You will be my greatest treasure, a reward for my patience." He cackled again. "Come to me, and I will let the wolves live. Well, maybe for a day or two." He laughed again as a helicopter blew up.

"Fools, they only give us more energy," one of the smaller demons said. "We've been planning this for centuries. Australia is one of the best places for an underground operation to go unnoticed

since the country is so young and not as populated as others are. It helps that it has the smallest werewolf population. Because of all that we have gone unnoticed for hundreds of years."

All the demons in hearing distance laughed. The biggest one came for her, stabbing Jack's heart as he stalked her.

Faith came out of the vision screaming. Her eyes swept frantically around the room, and when they landed on Jack, she shoved out of Kane's arms, throwing herself toward Jack. "I…saw…I saw… You can't die! I will save you all." She would learn to advance her powers. They would win.

She clung to Jack like her life depended on it. Jack rocked her and smoothed her hair back. With her head swimming from the information the vision had just shown her, she tried to comprehend it all, then the world before her suddenly turned black and she passed out from exhaustion.

* * * *

Kane looked around his lounge room at the grim faces. Faith had never had a vision that had lasted that long. Usually the most she zoned out for was two to three minutes tops, and they were never unexpected anymore, she always felt them coming on. Today, though, she'd been out for about three hours.

Kane gazed at the pale, terrified, worried faces of his family members as they watched Faith. She had never come out of a vision screaming in terror or passed out afterward. He looked at his princess as she clung to his dad even in her unconscious state. His mother's face drained of color as she paced before the sofa, obviously debating what to do.

His dad looked up at Griffen who was sweating and white as a ghost. "What's she feeling? What did you get?"

Griffen slumped to the ground. "Not good, Dad, not good at all. I've never felt anything so powerful, and the worst thing was half of that was dark power."

His dad's brow furrowed. "What's she feeling now?"

"Drained, exhausted, terrified, but she's hanging in there. God, she's amazing."

His dad nodded in agreement and hugged Faith tighter. She sighed and relaxed her grip, and her breathing changed to a more relaxed sleeping pattern.

Kane went to his dad to take his mate. He and his wolf were edgy, and he needed to hold Faith, to know she was all right.

Jamie and Devlin stopped him. "You are not touching her. She isn't even with you twenty-four hours and look what happened. She has avoided you and not spoken to you in over four years. For crying out loud, to get her to come home we had to tell her you were seeing a woman who you were seriously considering mating and moving closer to the city with. When she does finally spend time with you, look what happens."

Devlin lifted Faith into his arms. Kane could see the love they had for her shinning in their eyes. Devlin turned to walk out of the house when Kane's wolf took him back over four years to that Halloween weekend, showing him the scenes again, with things he didn't want to remember. Kane doubled over, feeling sick as he relived what had happen when she stopped talking to him.

"I hurt her deliberately, hoping it would stop her following me like my shadow, but I did it more so she would stop loving me." He looked up into all their faces. "I wanted her to hate me, avoid me, and then maybe I would stop loving her instead of feeling like a cradle robber." He sighed. "She was sixteen, I was frigging thirty. It was the first time, though, that I really saw her for what she was to me, she was a real princess, and I knew she had chosen that outfit especially for me. I took one look at her and if I wasn't already in love with her I would have been. I had never felt like that before, and I was terrified. My God, you guys have to remember she looked stunning, like a fantasy princess. I couldn't take it, so I went to find the she-wolf I was seeing at the time. We were going at it in my room when I felt Faith coming. It was then for the first time I smelt her chocolate and vanilla scent. I heard her open the door, so I said 'I love you,' looking at the she-wolf. I heard Faith gasp then run away. I made it worse when I called Faith's name when I finished, which didn't go down well with the she-wolf. She left, but she went to go find Faith. I think I caught all the conversation, stuff about her only having a crush on me and me thinking of her as an annoying necessity, I think I even felt the pain from where I was hiding like a coward. Then the she-wolf said that I was alpha, next in line, and she was just a nobody human. I nearly broke then, my wolf wanted to kill the she-wolf, but I held back and as soon as the she-wolf was done I grabbed her and we left. I broke Faith's heart. That's why she has had nothing to do with me."

Jamie drew back his arm, punching Kane square on his nose. Pain exploded across his face, but it was nothing less than he deserved. "You're a fucking arsehole. I found her that day and it took me hours just to get her to stop crying, and I had to console her for weeks. She wouldn't even tell me what it was about." Jamie took Faith from Devlin and headed to the front door.

Devlin joined in by stepping up to Kane and slogged his nose, making it bleed. "I had no letters for two weeks. That was the only time I didn't get any besides when I was on missions. Shit, Kane, I thought someone had died. I almost went AWOL."

Devlin joined Jamie at the door, Griffen walked over to them. "Wow, Kane, I never knew you were so selfish. I had months of…I guess you could call it no sunshine, because every time I checked on everyone there was a void where Faith usually was. Somehow, she had learned to block me. When I asked about it she said she wasn't feeling good and she'd blocked me so I didn't feel bad."

Kane was shocked when even Rane got up. "Well, we all know why she stopped talking to you. Faith knew you knew what happened and what was said. She probably knew you were watching, hiding." Rane shook his head. "You really are an arsehole, and now you expect her to just get over what you did to her. You could have done something to fix the rift over the years, but no, after all this time you expect her to just happily be your mate."

Even Arden shook his head as he got up to join them. They walked out the door with Faith while Kane sat on his lounge, scared that what Rane had said was true. He was so angry with himself.

"Really, son, there were other ways," said his dad.

His mum took his hands in hers. "Look, we're not perfect, no one is, but I really think you need to give her some time. She was sixteen, and that's such a vulnerable age. I know she's twenty now, but we all knew how she felt. My God, Kane, she must still have feelings for you or she would never have stayed last night."

He tried to say she had no choice but his mum wouldn't let him get a word in.

"I know you don't think she could have stopped you, but I remember watching her train with all of you and she never lost a fight. Ah, don't say you all let her win, because I remember a couple of visiting wolves who spared with her and they all started taking it easy on her 'til the end and they still ended on the floor. So don't give me that she had no choice. She stayed last night because she wanted to. Give her some time. Call her later to organize a time to talk and woo her. Your father and I are going now too, so think about it."

Kane was left in his large house all by himself.

* * * *

Faith had awoken when Kane was telling everyone what she walked in on. He then told them what the girlfriend had said to her. Faith was so embarrassed she didn't say anything for the whole ride back to her parents' house. She turned to all five guys as they got out of the car.

"I'm sorry for the four years of childish behavior I put you all through, but at first I was so upset and angry that I couldn't even look at him, and then it just became easier to give him what he wanted. So I left him alone. It hurt too much when I was around him anyway." Faith wiped her tears away. "It really does seem silly and immature now that I think about it and hear it out loud."

They enveloped her in a hug.

Rane pulled her face up and said, "You were only sixteen and thought you were giving him what he wanted."

She smiled. "I love you all."

Jamie gave her a bear hug.

Rane shocked her by saying, "How about we all do something fun later tonight?"

Faith smiled. "Thanks, but I said I would go to Splash tonight with Remy and Sara. I promised I would join them in a competition. I love you all, but I need some girlfriend time. I'm going to go write in my vision book. I promise I'll tell you what I saw tomorrow. Hey, aren't you guys supposed to be out tonight saving the world?"

They all laughed. "You sure you're okay?" Devlin

asked. "We could come in and keep you company 'til your friends come to pick you up."

"*No!*" Fuck, she said that too loud and too quickly. She backtracked before one of them offered to be the designated driver. "No, thanks. Really, I'm fine. We're just going to go out dancing for an hour or two. So, I'll see you tomorrow." She ran inside before they asked any more questions.

Faith knew she was being selfish not telling them the information she saw in her vision instead of going out with her friends. The werewolves would die if they knew what she was doing tonight. Faith shuddered at the thought of how they would react if they saw her, but she was going to do this, not just for fun but to help build some much needed confidence again, especially now that she was back with all the gorgeous wolves. Tonight was going to be hers. She was going to get dressed up in something sexy, get drunk, dance, and basically behave like a normal twenty-year-old. No overprotective wolf around. She would worry about saving the world tomorrow.

Chapter 3

Kane felt like shit. He knew he needed to talk to Faith, apologize, beg her to forgive him. But like the coward he was, he sat in his huge, empty house watching the afternoon sun turn into night. Kane's wolf was hounding him to go get their mate, bring her back home, make her believe he was sorry and they loved her.

Kane frowned. Did they, did he, really love her? What he'd done to her wasn't the actions of someone in love. He had known her for fifteen years, well over half her life. Faith wasn't perfect by any means, but he had watched her grow into a remarkable woman, well teenager, since she hadn't had anything to do with him for over four years. What he had learned and found out, he really liked. He'd loved her four years ago, and after last night there was no denying he still loved her. Last night had been amazing. He still couldn't believe his beautiful princess had been a virgin, because she drew people to her, especially men. His wolf had been ecstatic that he would be her one and only.

Kane stood up and walked to his shower, thinking of ways to make up with her. Faith had said she didn't love him anymore, but he knew she did, otherwise she wouldn't have let anything happen last night. There would be a lot of things to sort and figure out. It wouldn't be easy, but Faith was worth it. He was so lucky to have her as his true mate.

He got dressed and drove to her house to find his princess.

* * * *

Kane tried Faith's mobile again, then Jamie's, Devlin's, and he even tried Griffen's mobile, but no one picked up. Faith's parents hadn't been any help, all he got from them was that she had gone out with friends. So he tried his parents for info because he was starting to get an uneasy feeling, his wolf was pacing.

He finally got in contact with his mum who just said to remember her advice and try Rane. So Kane tried Rane's mobile. He picked up on the first ring, and Kane sighed in relief. Kane could hear loud music in the background.

"Where are you? Do you know where Faith is?"

There was a long silence. "Kane, give her a rest tonight."

"Please, Rane, I do love her, and I need to apologize."

There was a sigh that could barely be heard over the music. "I'm just about to enter a nightclub in the city called Splash."

"What, why?"

"Because that's where Faith and her friends are. I thought I would keep watch, make sure she's safe."

"Rane, that's my job. She's my mate."

"Yeah, well, how about you let her cool down tonight, see her tomorrow. I'll keep her safe."

Kane really didn't have a good feeling. He was already in his car, pushing it to the limits. "Why the fuck is your voice edgy?"

"Ah, I just bumped into three of our brothers. Looks like they had the same idea."

The music got louder and he could hear cheering. "I'll be there in five to ten minutes."

"Kane, stay at home. There are four of us... Holy shit."

Kane could hear Jamie in the background saying, "That is not our princess, that is a hot sex kitten." It was followed by four growls.

"What the fuck is Jamie going on about?"

Rane cleared his throat. "Ah, Kane, I really do think it's best if you stay home tonight and talk to Faith tomorrow. We've got it covered from here."

"I was already heading to the city to her friends, I'll—"

"Shit, I gotta go, Kane."

Rane disconnected the call, and Kane chucked his phone in the passenger seat.

What the hell was going on? Kane sped up, not liking the sound of what he'd heard.

* * * *

Faith was having so much fun she didn't even notice the four massive, slack-jaw werewolves that came in the club until she and her two girlfriends were called up to the bar to be told they were the last contestants and would be going on next. Faith was pumped. The dance routine was one they had practiced, but had never been game to show.

Five minutes later, standing up on the stage bar, she glanced at the brothers, and they did not look happy. She thought about pulling out, but Remy and Sara were counting on her, they needed the prize money. Faith knew her werewolves wouldn't do anything in a crowded club with so many people watching. She gave a mental shrug. Stuff it, if she was going to be in trouble she might as well give them something to be mad about. Faith leaned down to the DJ coordinator. "On the second song, about two and a half minutes in, hose us down."

She took off her sequin top as she had a white singlet underneath that showed off a pink belly ring that matched her pink and black lacy bra set. To complete the outfit she had tight jeans and knee-high, black, fuck-me boots. She had told the girls if they wanted to win the $2,000 prize money they were going to have to use some serious dance moves to make the crowd cheer loud. She had told them to dress accordingly.

Faith heard her friend give a nervous laugh. "Oh my God," said Remy. "We are so going to win. Look at you two." She hugged Faith. "Thanks so much for doing this, Faith. You used to be so shy and reserved, but jeez, two years overseas has turned you into a bad girl. You were so right, they are going to go wild with these white singlets when we get wet."

They laughed as the music started and all those dance lessons Faith had taken made themselves known.

Catcalls, whistling, yelling for numbers, and loud cheers filled the air. She chanced a glance at the four very angry werewolves that were getting closer. A minute or two before the water hose was put on them she felt Kane and knew he had come in. Oh shit, she was dead. When she went down to slide across the bar, swapping spots with her friends for the finish of the song, she looked up to see the scariest sight she had ever seen—a six and a half foot massive, hulking, pissed off alpha werewolf stalking toward her. She gulped and rushed to follow her friends to the DJ.

* * * *

Kane had steam coming out of his head! What the hell

had happened to his princess? In her place was a vibrant, young sex kitten. He smiled a feral smile as his mind conjured up all kinds of things. He loved his princess or, he thought, sex kitten, but tonight there were going to be a lot of human male deaths, especially if one more man tried to touch her.

The crowd parted easily for him, sensing the danger coming off him. He was almost at the bar when he heard the human male next to him say to his friend, "What I wouldn't give to have a go at the one in the pink and black lacy bra and matching belly ring. Those exotic eyes are undoing me. I bet I could get her to come home with me. She looks like she could go all night."

Kane lunged for the human growling "mine" only to be grabbed by his brothers, who held similar expressions as him and were fighting to control themselves.

"Wait, it's almost done," said Rane through gritted teeth.

Griffen spat out, "Oh, she knew when you came in. She was scared shitless. Be prepared for her to do something crazy."

Kane chuckled, rubbing his hands together in anticipation of getting his hands and mouth on his new little sex kitten.

The music finished, and the cheers, whistles, and catcalls were deafening. The DJ talked about the end of the contest and how it looked like the final contestants were the winners, and he asked them to come and introduce themselves and get their prize money. Faith and her friends moved together over to the microphone and collected the check.

"What are your names?" the DJ asked.

The girls answered, "Sara, Remy, and Faith."

The DJ nodded. "Now, girls, what every guy out there, and quite possibly some girls, are wondering is are you single?"

They all laughed. Kane's eyes never left Faith's.

Remy said, "Yes, I'm single, and I'm ready for some fun."

Sara spoke up, "Sorry, boys and girls, I'm taken."

The DJ turned the microphone on Faith. Kane held his breath.

"Yes, today I'm single."

The crowd cheered as the three girls were carried off the stage. Kane's brothers let go of him, and he stalked to Faith. He turned her to face him, lifted her over his shoulder, said goodbye to her friends, and walked out the exit.

"Put me down, Kane. I can walk."

"Well, at least you didn't call me Dr. Wolfen." He sighed, pulled her around the corner of the building, and moved her to face him. "Look at me, Faith, because I'm only going to say this once. You are mine, my mate, my wife, never will you be single again. Wolves mate for life, and you're it for me. I have a ring for you at home, will you please wear it? The next time someone asks you if you're single, you will answer appropriately. Do I make myself clear, because wolves are a jealous, possessive lot with their mates." He cupped her face and kissed her gently. "I love you. I always have and always will. I can't live without you anymore."

Faith closed her eyes and rested her forehead against his. "I hate you right now. But you know what shits me off the most is no matter what I did or how hard I tried..." She looked up into his eyes. "I never stopped loving you."

She placed her mouth on his and started to kiss him, gently and shy at first, but then she traced his lips with the tip of her tongue and the kiss heated up. She nipped his bottom lip, and he growled and took over.

Faith pulled away at the clearing of throats. "So, there is one brother missing. Is Arden hiding somewhere?"

Kane chuckled. "I'm sure he would have been here too,

but someone has to work. Although I'm betting he and the rest of them are close by." He frowned. "Faith, what the hell were you thinking? You know demons focus on the paranormal."

* * * *

Faith groaned and tried not to get angry. Especially after the vision she had today, she knew that he was just protecting her. She took a deep, calming breath and started to answer him when another vision came at her.

> *Two young girls in scraggly, ripped clothing. One was about four or five, the other seven or eight. They sat hiding, covering each other's mouths, tears streaming down their dirty faces. They looked to be in some abandoned warehouse. Faith felt it wasn't far from where she and her werewolves were. She tried to look around for anything that could give away where they were. The place was filled with boxes, crates, and equipment that Faith didn't recognize. Then she saw a storage container with Black's Boating written on the side. Faith felt a direction of*

where they were toward the wharf.

The younger of the two started whimpering. Faith got a strong whiff of sulphur smoke as two demons and some minions came in.

"Come out, come out, wherever you are. We won't hurt you. Your daddy was a bad boy hiding you two from us because you're special."

Faith snapped out of the vision with a feeling of urgency. She was in Kane's arms, and Rane, Griffen, Devlin, and Jamie surrounded them.

She pushed against Kane's chest. "We need to go now." Kane let her go, instantly alert, scanning the area, but as soon as he let her go she started running in the direction she had a feeling the children were. "We need to get there now. Hurry."

The five werewolves followed. Kane picked her up and ran to where she pointed as he could run faster thanks to being a werewolf.

"I saw a storage container that said Black's Boating, but they're too far from the water to be safe." She couldn't stop shaking. She was terrified for the little girls, tears streaming down her face.

"Princess, you have to tell us what you saw."

"Two demons, minions, up ahead. Quick, we have to save the little girls," she called out.

Kane stopped and put her down, his face grim. "Are you sure it was two demons together? Demons always work alone."

She nodded. "No mistaking. You need to hurry."

"Point us in the direction. You go with Jamie."

"No, no, I can't. Two little girls need me, I must go. They're special, like me, and you need Jamie, there're two demons."

Kane seemed to silently debate for a second. "You can be two warehouses away, but you will stay back and with Jamie, only come over when he gives the all clear." He turned to Jamie. "Keep her away from the action, no matter what she says or does. I mean it, Jamie. Now that we're this close, I really don't have a good feeling, so stick to her like glue."

Jamie nodded. They continued on until they reached a section of run-down warehouses. Faith closed her eyes and pointed. All the werewolves took a deep breath.

"Fuck, I think she's right about there being two demons."

They ran in the direction she had pointed. Kane stopped and turned back, looking her straight in the eyes. "I mean it, Faith, no rushing in to save the day. Wait 'til Jamie gives the okay."

She nodded and tucked her arms around herself.

Kane was just out of sight when Jamie said, "You know you don't have to be with him, Faith."

She raised her eyebrow at Jamie.

"Just because you're his true mate doesn't mean you have to be with him. You're human."

Faith winced. She hated it when they said human like it was a dirty word.

"Don't do that, you know I didn't mean it that way."

She looked up into his bright green eyes. "This really isn't the time to discuss this, but for what it's worth, Jamie…" She looked up to see about fifteen minions coming toward them. "Fuck. Minions."

* * * *

Kane and his brothers ran in the direction of the sulphur smoke smell. He tried his best to keep his thoughts off Faith. He knew she was safe with Jamie, he was one of their best fighters, even at his young age. Not only that, she had trained with them since she was six through to her teen years. He had taught her some moves himself, and she even had specially made knives with iced tips. It also helped, he told himself, that he didn't smell sulphur smoke in her direction.

As they got closer, the brothers spread out to all sides of the building. Kane found the ball lighting rip that was a portal to the demon realm. It looked no bigger than a grapefruit, but Kane knew better as most demons were about ten to sixteen feet with massive muscles. He chanted the closing spell, and Rane came up beside him and put his blade through it to make sure they got all of it.

"My bad feeling is getting worse," Kane said. "It's too quiet, and where are the minions?"

Just as he said that, six minions flew from the roof to attack them. The gray pig-like creatures with sharp claws and even sharper teeth, which they used to eat flesh, were only about four and a half feet tall. They were easy to dispose of by ripping or cutting their wings off, chopping their heads off, then pulling out their hearts.

Kane and Rane disposed of the minions easily, too easily, without even half-changing, something didn't feel right. They rushed inside to see a huge fifteen foot demon and a smaller one, about eleven feet tall. They both had gigantic black horns and huge thorns sticking out of their solid muscle with big, black eyes and bright red skin. The smaller demon had Griffen with both hands while Devlin dealt with his thick, long tail with the arrow-pointed end.

Rane and Kane half-changed which made them grow an extra three feet and bulk up. They became covered in protective fur over their extra-large human bodies.

The larger demon laughed as Rane and Kane showed up, the sound like nails scratching a chalkboard.

"Look who's come to join us, the great and powerful alpha here to save the day. I have to say I'm surprised you left your pretty little mate unprotected. Ah, Lucifer will be so happy. He has wanted to get his hands on one of the most powerful soothsayers in this century."

Kane tried not to react or show his surprise at the demon knowing so much, but he must have failed because the demon laughed again and then kicked Griffen out of the other demon's hands. Griffen flew across the room and hit the wall.

"We have our own soothsayer. She's not even a tenth of what your little mate is, but it doesn't matter, after tonight we will have her."

The demons attacked. As Griffen came up beside Rane, the demons used their horns to ram into them. Kane dodged but still got one in the shoulder. He used his extended claws to rip out the horn and grabbed his knife. It was a lot smaller than what he usually used, but in his rush to find Faith he only had the knife that he'd strapped in his boot. No werewolf went anywhere without an ice knife.

All four werewolves circled the demons. They needed to cut the tail first, as it did the most damage with its easy movement. They attacked together, Devlin and Griffen attacking the tails while Rane climbed on the big one's back. Kane distracted the demons from the front, focusing on the biggest one so Rane could get the head off. Griffen chopped the tail off and came to help Kane as he was caught in the demon's muscular, thorn-covered arms. Kane yelled to Griffen to help Devlin, who was struggling by himself with the smaller demon. His howl of pain as the demon cracked all his ribs was cut off as Rane chopped one of the demon's arms off. Kane fell to the floor. He got up, wincing, going straight for the heart of the demon who was bucking, trying to get Rane off, his remaining hand clawing at him.

Kane growled as he stuck his knife into the demon's black heart. He pulled it out then used the iced tip of his blade to shatter the heart as it tuned to ice. Kane moved out of the way quickly as the demon's body fell to the ground. The head rolled past him. Demons could live without a heart for a couple of hours but not their heads.

Kane turned to check on Devlin and Griffen's progress. He nodded to Rane to help, knowing he needed to get to Faith and Jamie. As he ran in the direction of his princess, he yelled, "I need to get to Faith and Jamie. Rane, you stay and find the girls Faith was talking about, and call for a cleanup crew. Tell Devlin and Griffen to join me."

Rane nodded and Kane changed into wolf form as it was faster to get to Faith. He prayed to all the gods that he would get there in time.

Chapter 4

Thank God she had been brought up with wolves, because she'd had it drilled into her since she started training with the boys to never leave home without one of your ice knives or blades. Faith reached down to her boot and pulled out her ice knife just as the first minion attacked, biting her arm, its thorny wings cutting her up. She cut the ugly creature's bat-like wings off and kicked another that was coming at her. She cut heads off and wings. Each time more came at her they bit and scratched her with their wings.

Jamie was surrounded by the rest of them. She screamed as a zombie came out of nowhere and grabbed her hair. She cut off its hand as another grabbed her around the waist. She hated zombies, because they used to be humans, but a demon had sucked the life and soul out of them. She kicked and stabbed its arms. Using its chest, she flipped out of its arms and landed not so well in front of it. Faith cut off its head. Shit, she was out of practice.

Grabbing a minion by the wings, she sliced them off as another bit her legs. Then she smelled sulphur smoke, and she turned in the smell's direction. Jamie had just killed the last minion and zombie, and his face paled at the sight of the thirteen foot hulking demon charging toward them. Faith felt Kane and knew he wasn't far.

"I feel Kane, he's not far, so we have to distract him. Come on, Jamie, snap out of it."

He growled and nodded, changing to his half-change form that made all werewolves an extra three feet taller. The demon reached them and Jamie pushed her behind him as the horn went through his chest. She heard the rib bones cracking, and without thinking, she ran around and climbed up the demon's back. She chopped the arrowhead tail off as it embedded in her arm. She screamed when more minions attacked her, trying to pull her off the demon's back.

Faith climbed further up the demon's back, using the thorns. She had to concentrate on holding on because her blood was everywhere, making it slippery. She heard the growl just as she reached the thick neck. The demon was bucking, and one of his clawed hands came around to help the minions pull her off. Faith slashed and kicked while trying to hold on for dear life.

She saw Kane pull up to a stop, change to half-change, do a quick assessment of the situation, and go to the front to help Jamie.

The demon yelled, "You will never be safe. I will not

die, we want her. She will be ours."

He tried to fall to the ground to squash Jamie and Kane. She knew Devlin had joined the fight, helping Jamie cut chunks in the demon's side and killing the minions, which helped Faith concentrate on cutting the head off, but her knife wasn't big enough. Devlin passed up his long blades. She reached, grabbing them and slicing her hands as she moved them up. The knives weighed a lot more than hers, so she focused all her strength on cutting the demon's head off. She knew his heart had been ice and it shattered when, using the last of her strength, she hugged his neck, pushing the blade toward herself. The demon tried bucking her off one last time, but it was too late. His head fell to the concrete. As she backflipped to the ground, the demon's body fell next to her landing spot.

She turned as strong, familiar arms picked her up. Boy, did he look pissed.

"What the fuck were you thinking, Faith, jumping up on a demon's back? You're covered in burns from his acid blood, and you're losing a lot of blood from the deep gashes you have. You're human."

She turned her face away from him as tears ran down her cheeks. God, how she hated that word.

"You will heal quickly, but not as fast as us. Shit, the

only reason that you survived at all was because when you mated with me you gained healing and strength. I could have lost you. You stupid girl, I can't ever lose you again."

She cried, her shoulders shaking as he started to walk with her.

"I love you, princess, and you said you wouldn't play hero."

Faith froze in his arms, looked into his eyes. "What did you just say? Do you really mean it? I know you said it earlier but..."

Kane stopped walking and looked at her face. He frowned. "I'm sorry, princess, I'm an arse, but you scared me to death when I saw you on the back of that demon." He shook his head. "Let's just say if werewolves could have a heart attack I would have had one. I can't live without you anymore, I love you."

Faith didn't care about the cuts, blood, and bruises. She reached up and pulled his mouth down to hers and kissed him. "I love you too. I will move in and give you a chance."

He smiled. "Let's get you cleaned up so I can see if we'll need to stitch you. The cleanup crew should be at the warehouse." He took off her bloody and holey singlet top. "Your jeans probably saved your legs from a lot of the burns."

Faith shut her eyes and leaned into him, breathing in his familiar sent. She snapped her eyes open and yelled, "The little girls!" She looked at Kane. "Who's looking for the girls?"

"Rane is looking for them."

She punched him, grimacing as the cuts bled again. "You idiot. I love Rane, but he's huge and scary as hell."

Faith jumped out of his arms, wincing as every bruise and cut made themself known, and started jogging in the direction of the warehouse she knew the girls were in. Once there she began to sing *Twinkle, Twinkle, Little Star* out loud, and repeated it.

After the second time Kane asked, "Why are you singing that song?"

"Their dad used to sing it to them. To tell them everything was going to be all right he told them whoever knew the song was good and would help them if they ever got in trouble." She stopped and turned to Kane. "I have an idea. Change into your wolf form before we round the corner."

He nodded. Faith started singing again. "*Twinkle, Twinkle, Little Star*," but in between she would say, "Aren't you a good doggie? You're my protector. Good doggie." She leaned down and whispered, "Bark like a dog."

His wolf huffed. Wolves did not like to be compared to dogs, they thought they were superior. He barked and Faith praised him.

"You are such a good doggie. You and my other doggies saved me from the monsters."

After about ten minutes of this, a scraggly little redhead popped out from behind some crates, next came a smaller, brown topped head. They slowly came out from hiding, walking toward Faith and Kane cautiously.

Faith smiled. "Hi. Do you like dogs? I have lots of doggies. This one is called Kane. There's another around here you might have seen, and his name is Rane."

Rane came in wolf form around the corner. Faith collapsed on the floor, wincing as the bruises and cuts made themselves known again. The wolves came to help her sit up, and she gripped Kane's fur as she put her arms around their necks.

"See, my doggies are protectors. They look after me and only hurt the monsters. They're really big, soft teddy bears." She buried her face in their necks.

Muffled laughter could be heard now from outside, damn wolf hearing.

The two frightened girls slowly moved forward until they were just out of arm's reach. Faith smiled. "Hi, my name's Faith. Let me introduce you to Kane and Rane."

The youngest little brown headed girl giggled. The redhead said, "They're funny names, they sound the same. They look the same too, how do you tell the difference?"

Faith laughed and kissed Kane's head. "You're absolutely right there…argh, I don't know your name. As I said, my name's Faith. What's yours?"

The redhead looked down at her feet and mumbled, "Grace."

"Well, Grace, they have lots of differences, you just have to come a little closer to see them. For example, Rane is just a smidgen smaller than Kane."

The girls took two tiny steps closer.

Faith continued, "Plus, Kane's fur is more a dirty blond where Rane's is tree bark brown."

The girls took another step forward.

Faith turned to the youngest. "What color doggie would you like…sorry, I know Grace's name but not yours, so can you tell me your name?"

The little girl grinned. "Sophie."

"Sophie, I almost have a rainbow of dogs, so what color doggie would you like?"

Sophie took the last step to Faith. "I want a white snow doggy with big water-colored eyes. As you know, the monsters don't like water or cold things. We tried to get close to water, but we must have still been too far. Did you go in the water? Is that why you don't got a shirt?"

Faith smiled. "You're right, Sophie, the monsters don't like water, and you were just a bit too far from the water. My shirt got wrecked helping fight the monsters, but don't you worry about that, I have lots of clothes at home. So let's find you a doggy protector. I have the perfect one for you. His name is Griffen, and he's even more of a teddy bear than these two."

There was a whole lot more laughter outside now as Griffen came in slowly. Sophie gasped and ran to Griffen, petting and hugging him as she chanted, "I love you. You're going to be my best friend and save me and my sister from the monsters. I bet they'll be scared of you, because you're the color of snow and your eyes are blue like water."

Griffen plopped down in front of Faith.

Grace sat down next to her sister, tears running down her face. "I wish we'd had a doggie protector so I could have saved our dad."

"I'm so sorry, Grace, but you can have a protector now."

"But I don't have anywhere to keep it now. My dad's gone, and I don't have a Mum anymore either." She was crying so hard it was tough to hear the last bit.

Faith moved over and hugged the girl. "Would you like to join my special family?"

Sophie stopped kissing Griffen to say, "Me too, me too. Grace and I are always supposed to be together, that's what Dad said."

Grace nodded. "Okay, but can I have a Mummy doggy, please?"

Faith smiled at them. "Ah, sweetheart, I can get you one of those, lat—" Suddenly a beautiful black wolf with brown eyes came running in and licked Grace's face. Faith nodded to Della, Kane's mother. "This is a Mummy dog. She's come to check on her babies."

Grace and Sophie looked around and as one said, "I don't see any babies."

"Why, we're hugging her biggest babies. Do you want to know something? These are only three of her babies, she has ten all up."

"Wow."

"Would you like to come with me and meet her other babies?"

Both girls nodded.

"Okay, kiddos, we're going to go outside. There will be some people, and more doggies. But we're going to go to a big white van."

Both girls nodded again. Faith moved slowly, trying not to wince so she didn't scare the girls further. She got up, leaning on Kane and Rane, and started limping, walking slowly to the exit.

* * * *

Kane knew Faith was about to collapse so he didn't care when Jamie came over to them and picked Faith up. She made a weak protest about Jamie being hurt. His response was to kiss her forehead.

"You're lighter than a feather."

Jamie then put on his, as Faith called it, lady-killer voice and turned to the two little girls.

"So I hear we have two new family members."

And as all females do around Jamie, apparently all ages, the girls constantly darted glances at him, giving shy smiles and moving as close as they dared.

"Why are you carrying Faith?" Grace asked. "She's not a baby, put her down now." The little girl even stomped her foot for effect.

Jamie chuckled. "It's so nice to have another hotheaded redhead around."

As usual Jamie had cast his spell, and Grace seemed to forget she was telling him off. She smiled, saying, "My daddy always said us redheads have to stick together."

Jamie snickered and gently placed a sleeping Faith in the middle seat so the girls could sit on either side. Griffen, Rane, and his mother hopped in after the girls. Kane, still in wolf form, joined them, and Jamie hopped in behind them.

His father Jack drove toward home.

"Do you have a doggie protector, Jamie?" Grace asked.

"Yes, I do, and he is red."

"You must live in a house with a big backyard. We lived in a flat."

"Yes, I have a two bedroom house."

"What about Faith? Does she live with you? Because that sounds small for all us and her doggies."

"Well, Faith just got back from a big holiday and hasn't decided where or who she is going to live with."

Kane growled at his idiot brother as the girls started to cry. Faith startled awake at the noise and listened to the girls.

"She has to have a place, she said we could come live with her and be part of her family."

Faith, who even in her tired state was on the ball, answered, "Silly Jamie. I live in a big, five bedroom house overlooking the water."

The girls clapped and the tears instantly stopped.

"That's so good, Faith, because the monsters don't like the cold or water. Right?" said Sophie.

"You're right, they don't."

The three girls fell asleep shortly after. Faith awoke as Kane picked her up and moved her inside. Jamie and Jack grabbed a girl each and placed them in the bedroom next to Kane's. Della and Griffen followed, still in wolf form, and jumped on the bed, curling up on each side of the girls.

Kane took Faith to their room where he took the rest of her clothes off, carried her into the bathroom, filled the tub with water, and placed her in the warm bath. She winced and clung onto him tightly. He reached into his doctor's bag and did what he could. Kane looked Faith in the eyes.

"I'm so proud of you. What you did for those girls, how you handled them… I'm in awe of you, princess. I think, if at all possible, I fell even more in love with you."

Faith smiled, she seemed too tired to speak.

"I'm going to give you something to help the pain. It will also help you sleep through the night."

He picked an exhausted Faith out of the bath, dried her, and put her into bed.

Chapter 5

After putting Faith to bed Kane joined his father and some of his brothers in the lounge room.

"We have a huge problem. Those three demons were working together. They also knew things about us they shouldn't have," Kane said as he stared at his father and brothers.

His father and Arden shook their heads. "Are you sure, Kane? Demons are loners, they have never been seen together or worked together before."

Rane answered, "Well, these sure did, and they knew we were coming, but not who or how many of us there would be."

"They even knew Faith. One demon said he was surprised Kane left her behind and she is one of the most powerful soothsayers in this century."

Shock showed on Arden's and his father's faces.

Kane sighed. "We need to have a pack meeting. We also need to get in contact with the alphas of other packs. It sounded like they want Faith, so she needs a guard, which she will definitely not like."

His dad raked his fingers through his hair. "We also

need to find out Faith's vision. I have a feeling it will be very useful information. I say we organize a pack meeting for tomorrow afternoon. By then we should have as much info as we need. Let's all go home and be back bright and early in the morning. Ah, before I forget, Kane, I got Ava and Eve to pack some of Faith's clothes and put them in your room. They also told her parents were she was."

With that last comment everyone left and Kane joined Faith in bed.

* * * *

Faith stretched, snuggling into Kane some more. She had the feeling she was being watched and not by Kane. She snapped her eyes open to two pairs of eyes staring at her, muffled giggles, and pointing. She elbowed Kane who shot awake bare chested. The girls giggled even louder.

"Hi, Grace and Sophie. Is everything all right?" Faith asked, making sure the sheet covered her naked body.

"We're hungry, and the sun is out. Can we have breakfast?"

Faith sighed, looking around for something better to cover herself with. "Sure. I'll get up, just give me a minute."

Sophie jumped up and down. "Do you have Coco Pops? That's my favorite. Faith, do you know you have a man in your bed? Are you married? Because my daddy said boys and girls don't sleep in the same bed unless they're married." Sophie stopped jumping and looked at Faith's bare fingers. "You don't have a ring on your finger, did you lose it?"

Faith stared at the little girl. How on earth did she get all that out in one breath?

Kane chuckled beside her. He reached into his bedside top drawer and pulled out two diamond rings. One of the rings had a row of six stones, alternating between ocean blue stones and diamonds. The second ring had a massive diamond that fit into the slight curve of the first ring. They were beautiful, and all Faith could do was stare, mouth agape.

Kane picked up her left hand and placed them on her finger. Of course they were a perfect fit. He kissed her fingers and placed a light kiss on her lips. "I love you." He then turned to the girls, proceeding to tell them, "Yes, Sophie, you are completely right. Faith wasn't wearing her rings last night because she helped fight the monsters."

This seemed to be an okay explanation, so the girls asked together, "What's your name?"

Kane chuckled again. "I'm Dr. Kane Wolfen."

The girls' eyes grew wide. "Faith has a doggie

protector named Kane!"

He smiled at them. "Yes, yes she does."

"Our doggie protectors went outside, we think to do their morning things," Sophie informed them.

Grace added, "Is that where your other doggies are, Faith?"

Faith laughed. "They're probably with their families, playing. So why don't we let them play while we have breakfast? Go to the toilet, and don't forget to wash your hands and face, and I'll meet you in the kitchen, okay?"

The girls nodded enthusiastically and ran out of the room arguing over who got to use the toilet first.

Kane smiled at her. "You're so beautiful, especially with those girls. I'm going to give a buddy of mine a call later. He deals with children of abuse and violence. It would be good if we got some professional advice as those girls have been through a lot. He can tell us what he thinks we should do."

She nodded, knowing it was the best option.

Faith sat, not caring about her nakedness now that the girls were gone. She turned to look at Kane lying in bed. He looked so hot it took her breath away. His dirty blond hair was everywhere, he was probably due for a haircut, but she loved it. It made her want to lean down and run her hands through it.

Kane's ocean blue eyes that matched her ring still looked sleep-dazed. She moved her gaze over his very well-defined eight-pack chest, and her breathing started to pick up. She would swear her pussy was drenched. Her gaze traveled further down. There was no mistaking his morning delight.

Kane growled. Jumping out of bed, he picked her up and carried her into the bathroom. He locked the door, putting her against it.

"I can smell you. God, you smell so good."

He leaned his face down, lifting her so he could lick her pussy, and they both moaned.

"Fuck, if there weren't two little girls out there waiting patiently for their breakfast and half of my family about to let themselves in I would lick and suck you until you couldn't take any more."

Her head fell back against the door. He moved back up her body and fastened his mouth to hers. His hand moved down and he slowly put a finger in her pussy. He growled.

"Princess, you're soaking wet."

He placed her on his dick, and he had gotten her so worked up he slid in easily. He walked over to the shower, his movements making his cock go in and out. She covered her moan by biting him.

Kane growled loudly as he turned on the water taps. "Fuck it. Jamie is out there, he has them sorted out."

Kane then put them in the shower, her up against the wall. "Look at me, princess. I love to watch you come, I've never seen anything hotter." He looked into her eyes as he moved.

She wrapped her legs around him. "Kiss me, Kane."

He placed one gentle kiss on her lips then he traced them with his tongue. Faith opened her mouth and her tongue met his. She moaned as his hands moved to her breast. He circled her nipples with his fingers and pulled just enough to make her scream her orgasm into his mouth. She stared into his eyes that were shining with love and passion as he roared his own release. She smiled in satisfaction as his dick grew, locking him inside as he came.

"I don't think we thought this through. How long will you lock?"

He smiled. "I don't care how long, that was so hot. God, every time I touch you I burst into flames. It was definitely worth being locked for about twenty minutes."

He kissed her, then turned the shower off, wrapped a huge towel around them, and walked them to the bed. Each time he moved she moaned in ecstasy.

"What about the girls?" she asked.

"Jamie, Ava, and Eve have it sorted. Trust me, they know."

Faith blushed and buried her face in his chest. He kissed her head and rubbed her back.

* * * *

Twenty-five minutes later, Kane dressed and went to greet his family, who he found all playing the Wii console. His twin sisters turned around. "Where's Faith?"

"Why hello to you too, Ava and Eve. I'm good, thanks for asking."

They rolled their eyes.

"She'll be out in a minute." He sat on the lounge and waited for Faith.

Faith came out in a blue singlet and knee-length, black shorts, her hair in a messy bun. He was a lucky man. She was gorgeous. Faith came over and sat on his lap.

"Love you, princess."

She smiled and kissed his cheek. Kane felt a tugging on his sleeve, and he looked down to see Sophie.

"She said her name was Faith, not princess."

Kane smiled. "Well, I think she should change her name to princess, don't you? She is everything a princess should be. She's kind, caring, brave, and beautiful. Plus, she has a brave prince to rescue her."

The girls laughed. "Yes, and she has long hair like a princess. She's young too."

Kane winced at the last comment.

Sophie's eyebrows drew together and she pursed her lips as she added, "How come she married you, because you have got to be really old?"

Everyone laughed. Kane growled at the werewolves.

"I don't think I look that old."

The girls giggled and Grace spoke up. "Well, you don't have white hair or lots of wrinkles, but you said you're a doctor and all the doctors I know are old."

Sophie whispered loudly in her sister's ear, "Maybe he gave her magic medicine that made her marry him."

Even Faith laughed at that. Grace shook her head and whispered back, "No, silly, he has the magic medicine for himself so he doesn't look old, that way Faith, his princess, stays with him."

Sophie grinned at her sister. "You're so smart." She smiled at everyone laughing. "Can I go outside and play with the doggies now?"

"We're going to go shopping soon to get you some things, so how about we let them play, and you can play with them when we get back?"

The girls' faces fell. "We want to play not go shopping. All we ever get when we go shopping is food."

Faith smiled at them, and Kane would swear the sun shone brighter. "Well, this time we're going to get you girls clothes and toys."

They squealed at this and started jumping up and down. Kane leaned down to whisper in Faith's ear. "Princess, we need to talk about the last forty-eight hours."

She nodded. Kane turned her head and kissed her lips gently. She moved her hand up to his neck, and the kiss intensified. The world fell away until it was just the two of them, then reality came back too quickly at the sound of cleared throats and little girls' giggles.

He sighed. "I don't want you taking the girls out alone. I know it's daylight, but there're still zombies. It would make me feel so much better if you took Jamie."

Jamie groaned. "Argh, not shopping!"

"I would go, but I want to get in contact with that doctor friend I told you about, and meet with some of the elders who can't make it to the meeting tonight."

His mum and twin sisters piped up, "We'll go too. We love shopping."

Jamie groaned louder. "What did I ever do to deserve this kind of torture? Shopping with six females..." He shivered.

Kane laughed as Ava patted Jamie on the back. "You can be our bag boy."

They all laughed but Grace patted Jamie to get his attention. "Don't worry, I'll help you with the bags. Plus, you're really big so no one will ever pick on us. Also, us redheads have to stick together."

"Okay, looks like everything is settled. We'll all meet back here for dinner before the meeting," Kane said. He smiled at Faith. "Princess, we're going to have to know about that big vision you had yesterday."

She sighed. "All right, but I warn you all, you're not going to like what I have to say."

She kissed his lips lightly, grabbed her handbag, and helped the girls get ready to go.

After they left, Kane went straight to his parents' house where he found his father and two youngest sisters cleaning the yard. His father stopped, walking straight to him.

"You're just in time. I have three alphas calling me back so we can do a conference call together. I hate to say this, but it's sounding like the demons are getting smarter. I've spoken to the elders and none have ever come across three demons working together. It's making me a lot more nervous about hearing Faith's vision."

"You're right, Dad. I think we might have to ask for help. We're just not a big enough pack to deal with this."

* * * *

As they pulled into the shopping center car park Faith turned to Grace and Sophie.

"Now you girls know the rules, right? No running off. No talking to strangers. Do not leave our sights. Got it? If you have any questions don't be afraid to ask, especially if you need to go to the toilet. Lastly, how old are you?"

Grace frowned. "Seven, but I'll be eight in twelve days."

Faith winced. *Poor thing.* To go through everything she had and have only her sister left… Thank God they had found them.

Sophie smiled, adding, "I'm five, just turned five, I had a cake and everything."

Faith looked at the girls with tenderness. "That's great. Do you think you can remember the rules?"

The girls nodded. As they were getting out of the car Grace asked, "Can we go to the bag shop first where the big, red boy-man is waiting for us?"

All the wolves froze as Faith turned to Grace. "Do you know what the man wants to talk about, or how he knows we're here?"

Grace beamed up at Faith. "Yes, he knows what you are. He wants to help. The monsters call him half-breed. His mum told him to come here today." She seemed to come out of a trance. "How funny is that!"

Della nodded to Jamie and walked away, talking on the phone. Jamie smiled down at the girls. "Well, thank you, Grace, but I'm dying for some toys, so do you two want to go to the big toy store first?"

Both girls nodded, jumping up and down. "Toys, toys."

Faith grabbed the girls' hands. "Okay let's go. Which aisle should we take Jamie down first? Dolls, Barbie, costumes, teddy bears, or books?"

Jamie groaned. "I was thinking video games."

Both girls said, "No, Barbie dolls."

Faith laughed as they headed into the toy store. One hour later after the girls had filled a trolley each and were now in Jamie's favorite place, video games, Faith felt arms come around her waist. Turning her around, Kane kissed her neck, moving up to her cheek, and then he picked her up and their lips met.

She sighed into his mouth. Their kiss was cut off again by giggling and a "yuck" from Jamie followed by more giggling.

Kane leaned his forehead against hers. "I missed you."

Faith rolled her eyes. "You have done just fine without me for several years, I don't think two hours should worry you." She frowned. "So how many did you bring for this one guy who's supposed to want to help?"

"Grace said half-breed, so all we know is that this creature is red and big, I don't even want to think of what it could be. I do not like the feeling I'm getting, but I can't even fathom that those monsters could somehow breed with humans." Kane shook his head like he was trying to get rid of rotten thoughts. "To be safe, I brought four, then there's Jamie, Ava, Eve, Mum, and I."

At his overreaction, she moaned. "It's just one man. Plus, I don't have a bad feeling, and I haven't had any visions."

He kissed her again. "Better safe than sorry. Okay then, let's get this show on the road. Everyone's in position, don't acknowledge them, we're hoping this half-breed's sense of smell isn't as good as ours. I have Blake and Tray only two stores down. I'm going to stay with you. Jamie's going to be at our backs."

Faith nodded as they headed out of the toy store. Rane grabbed the trolley and put everything into his car. "Did you buy the whole toy shop?"

"No, silly, but we got lots more toys now than like

ever," Sophie said.

They walked into the shopping center.

Chapter 6

Faith turned to the girls. "We're going to go talk to that man now so I need you girls to listen."

They both nodded. Ava and Eve asked if they would like piggyback rides, which they enthusiastically accepted. Eight stores in was the bag store, and standing in front of it was a really tall man with dark skin. His clothes were baggy, and he had a hat on his head, hiding his features. He looked up and straight into Faith's eyes, and she gasped when she saw that his eyes were black with a red tinge around the edge. As she got closer she could tell his skin also had a red tinge.

Kane swore. Faith couldn't take her eyes off the stranger, there was something familiar about him.

"I don't feel any danger, Kane. I actually get really positive vibes."

The half-breed's eyes never left Faith, and the odd thing was that they looked on her with love. When she was only a shop away, he smiled, revealing long, sharp teeth. Kane snarled, and the man stopped smiling, covering his teeth. Faith could feel the menace, anger, and curiosity coming off the werewolves as they reached the bag store.

Kane stood in front of her.

"You don't look at her. If you have something to say, say it to me." Kane growled, flashing his sharp, lengthened teeth.

Faith knew Kane was being overprotective because they weren't sure what this half-breed demon could do. Demons had the ability to control you as long as you kept your gaze on them and didn't get distracted, and once they got their teeth into you and drained you of your blood, you became their zombie to command.

Faith carefully peered around Kane and noticed that the man looked a lot younger than she had originally thought. She didn't even think he was a man, more like a young teenager.

"She said you would be beautiful, and it would shine from the inside out. You look exactly like her," the half-breed said. He sounded like a teenager whose voice was just about to break.

A red tear fell from his eyes. He reached out to touch her, but quick as lightning, Kane grabbed his hand. "You don't ever touch her. Don't even look at her!"

The boy winced. "I would never hurt her, I love her. My mum said you werewolves would look after her."

Faith looked around. She had been so involved in

everything going on that she hadn't realized they had been walking to the exit, surrounded by the werewolves.

The half-breed continued, "She said her princess would always be protected. She knew they were coming for her, they wanted you. Mum said it was fate helping that that woman had a stillborn child." He looked at Faith and whispered, "They never knew. Mum bespelled you."

Kane growled and moved in front of Faith again. "Half-breed, I won't tell you again, don't look at her."

Faith frowned. "What are you talking about?"

She glanced around to see they were in the far end of the car park where there were only one or two cars.

"I'm half-breed to everyone, but Mum called me Ben, her big Bengie. Mum tried to come with me, but they killed her. She died so I could get here on time. Mum said to tell you she loved you with all her heart. She said when you touch me you would know all she said and you would love me just like she did." Red tears were rolling from his eyes. "I like the daylight, as you can see. I'm different from the demons. I ran here to you in the sun. I even like water. Mum said she couldn't see what would happen, but she knew I needed to be here and you would be here with your wolves, but the visions didn't show her how many there would be. She said it would be hard, but once you touched me you would know I'm your brother. My mum was your mum."

Rane and Blake grabbed Ben and started pulling him to a van.

"Please, just touch me and you'll know."

Faith knew she shouldn't do it, but she was the only paranormal psychic in her family, and she had always felt like the odd duck. She didn't look like either of her parents or their family, and she couldn't shake the feeling he was telling her the truth. Without thinking, she ran around Kane and touched Ben's hand. She heard Kane's roar of "noooo" as he grabbed her around the waist as the vision started.

> *A very pregnant woman who looked exactly like Faith waddled into the hospital. As she entered she yelled, "Please, my baby's coming. Please hurry, we don't have much time."*
>
> *Nurses ran to the woman, grabbing her just before she fell to the floor. They rushed her up in the elevator then along a corridor and into a room. The woman yelled, chanting some words that Faith didn't know. She screamed, moaned, and a baby girl came out squealing.*

The woman panted her thanks, kissing the baby and murmuring love words. Then she gave the baby to one of the nurses, grabbing her hand and saying, "I know what you are. You have to help me. They're coming for me and my baby. She's special. Please, there's a couple two rooms down, she's about to give birth to a stillborn baby girl. Switch them. I have bespelled her, they will think she's their child. In five or so years they will live near wolves but won't know it. The wolves will love my child and keep her safe. She will be important to all supernatural creatures if she lets herself be." The woman smiled. "She will even be mate to one. Please. Bring me the stillborn. I'll say she's mine. Quick, do it and get out of here before they get you too."

The nurse nodded and rushed away with the baby. The woman broke down, crying as she chanted. Five minutes later the nurse returned with the stillborn, and the woman shooed the nurse away.

"Run, go somewhere cold with lots of

snow or live near water. You must listen to me." The woman kissed the stillborn's head. "I'm so sorry."

A few minutes later four zombies arrived and took the woman away. They locked her in some kind of cell with no windows. Tears rolled down the woman's face as her torture began. Small demons came to her cell and forced themselves on her. She fought every time, never giving up, but it did no good. Over the years she fell pregnant many times but miscarried them all. They left her alone for a while and this time when a small demon came she didn't miscarry, she stayed pregnant.

By this time the woman was white and sickly looking. She screamed in agony as she gave birth. The baby was big, and she was in tremendous pain. She gave birth alone to a massive baby boy, at least a twelve pounder, with dark skin with a red tinge, a full mouth with sharp teeth, and black eyes with a red tinge.

The woman cleaned herself up and

then sung to the baby, saying, "You are my Ben, my Bengie boy. I love you. Always remember that you're special, just like your sister. You will be a good boy, don't listen to anyone who says otherwise." She sang this and told the baby about all the good things in the world, then a demon came in and took the baby. She fought but was no match for him.

Then Faith saw the little boy sneaking into her room, looking no more than two, bringing food and water. The woman hugged and kissed him, telling him stories of wonderful things she had seen. Then he hugged her and snuck back out.

Faith saw several of these incidents until finally Ben looked to be about the age he was now. The woman looked frail and lifeless.

Ben picked her up. "I did what you told me. They should all be passed out if they ate the food. I love you, Mum. We're getting out of here, and I'll get you to my sister."

The woman smiled. "I love you too, my special boy. Remember my instructions on where to go, and if anything happens to me, promise me you will keep going. Remember, find your sister, help protect her. Live life, have fun."

Ben shook his head. "No, Mum, I can't leave you."

"You must remember they need to get a werewolf army down here to save people. This place is only one of thousands. The wolves have to annihilate it and any others after saving the people. Promise me," his mum said.

Faith could see they were in some tunnels, heading up.

The woman moaned. "I love you." She jumped down just as they reached a door, opened it, and attacked the demon, yelling at Ben, "Run! Run for me." With the last of her breath she said, "I break thy power and give it to my children."

The last thing Faith saw before she came out of the vision was Ben bursting out of a door into the daylight.

Faith knew from the bottom of her heart that what she saw was true, she even felt it was the truth. Her whole life up until now had been a lie. She didn't know what to do. Should she feel grateful, pissed, loved, safe, special, or relieved? She now knew she had a brother, a half-brother but a brother, and her biological mother had died. She knew from the vision that her biological mother wanted her to look after, teach, and love Bengie. Faith started to silently sob, tears rolling down her cheeks, selfish tears for everything she had lost, but mostly because Ben got to know their mother.

Faith snuggled into Kane. His arms tightened around her as he whispered things to her, like he loved her and he didn't want to live without her, how sorry he was for the years they'd missed, and other silly nonsense about her childhood. She needed him right now. She was so scared, and she needed to know she was loved. She wanted to be reminded of who loved her and why.

"Wake up, princess. I love you. Please don't do this. Wake up. I promise I will give you anything you want, I'll even buy you that puppy you wanted. Remember that? We could never understand why you wanted one when you had all of us." He gave a harsh laugh. "I'll buy you two if you wake up now. Or how about I build you that princess chair and the castle that had to be bigger than everyone else's? We'll even make Jamie be the dragon again. I secretly think he liked that, probably has a costume in the closet already. Devlin won't complain when I, the prince, save him from the dragon. Do you know I never played games with any of the other children, not even my sisters or brothers? I always felt and said I was too old, but you would look at me with those warm, brown eyes, bottom lip quivering, and I would cave and do anything you said. God, I love you so much. Open your eyes, honey. I can't go back to my bleak existence of the last four years. I'll do anything."

Faith couldn't listen to any more, she opened her eyes and leaned up and kissed him. "I love you too. You always did like saving me from the dragon considering I had to trick you every time to play, and I want two chocolate Labradors."

Kane laughed and kissed her long and hard. "Don't ever do anything so stupid again, Faith. What the hell were you thinking? He's a fucking half-breed demon, the only one we know of. For Christ's sake, we didn't know it was possible they could breed with…argh, fuck, I don't even want to fathom it. If werewolves could have heart attacks you have almost given me two in less than forty-eight hours."

Then she broke down, crying. "What they did to my mother…oh God, Kane. Bengie's special, there are not many like him because they usually miscarry. My mum wants me to look after Bengie, teach him, love him. I think he's even younger than we think." She stopped and looked around their room for him. "Where is he?"

Faith glanced around the room again. Jamie was asleep in a chair, just coming awake now. Griffen was leaning against the wall, looking white as a ghost.

"Griffen, what's wrong?"

She tried to get up, to go to him, but arms tightened around her waist.

Griffen gave a forced smile as he said, "That vision of yours was pretty intense. I was stupid enough to touch you, and let's just say you shared, which should be impossible because werewolves are immune to magic other than their own. Wow, Faith, wow."

Faith's eyes widened. She had never shared a vision before.

Griffen nodded at her. "I know, but when you touched the half-breed you got your mother's transferred power. I'm so sorry. We should have stopped him from being anywhere near you."

Faith shook her head, still feeling numb from all she had seen. "Where's Bengie? I need to see him."

All three werewolves cleared their throats. "Well."

Kane spoke up. "We didn't know for sure what he had done to you, and Griffen wasn't stupid enough to touch you until a couple of hours ago."

"So?"

Kane mumbled, "We put him in the water manhole, and he's being guarded."

Faith screeched, "You what! How long have I been out? How long has he been down there?"

Kane sighed. "For the rest of the day yesterday and all night. It's now mid-morning."

Faith punched Kane. "You left my baby brother down there." She punched him again. "You let me go, Kane, or you will learn what the word pain means. I can't believe you."

"Now, princess, just think about—"

Faith kneed him in the balls and punched him again. Jumping off the bed and running for the door, she yelled, "I'm really pissed with you all. If any of you tries to stop me or even moves a step closer, you will be so sorry."

She bumped into Jack as she ran out of the room. His

arms started to come around her and without even thinking she repeated her actions, doing the same to him as she had done to Kane.

As she ran for the back door, she yelled, "None of you Wolfens better stop me or come near me 'til I get my brother, or so help me God, you will not like the outcome."

She ran on bare feet down the rocky path to the cliffs until her feet were so badly cut and bleeding it started to get slippery, and then she finally saw two guards.

One broke away and casually walked toward her. "Faith, what are you doing here? It's not—"

Knowing it was all about the surprise, she ran up to him, kicked his balls, and punched his stomach. "Sorry, Blake, but stay the fuck away from me and my brother." She picked up one of his small blades.

As she got closer the other werewolf went into fighting mode. He was new, she didn't know him. He must have arrived while she was away. She swore as he sniffed the air. Faith curled her lips up at the side and knew she had a feral smile. She had to use more dirty tactics, as she wasn't sure how long her warning would hold off Blake and she was out of practice.

"You really shouldn't touch me. I'm the alpha's mate. Get my brother out of the hole, and I won't hurt you."

The new wolf laughed. "Bitch, you are not tricking me." He came forward to grab her, but she blocked him.

"Jeez, you're not a smart one, are you? It's your funeral. Didn't you notice how Blake never yelled at me or retaliated? Trust me, I am the alpha's mate."

The new wolf paused for a second, which was all she needed. Faith wasn't going to take any chances with this werewolf. She had never heard a werewolf speak to a woman like this guy was to her, and no matter how focused on the battle a werewolf was they should be able to listen and take notice of those around them. Holding Blake's blade, she ran and stabbed him in the stomach, using his body to flip over him.

She ran the last steps to the manhole and yelled down to her brother, "You can climb out now, but be quick."

Once she could see his hand, she grabbed it and helped him out. Suddenly a half-changed wolf grabbed her around the waist with his claws. She screamed as he said, "You fucking bitch, you'll pay for that."

He went to throw her, but she used the blade to slash his hands. She kicked off his chest, backflipping off him. Blake was running over and yelling at the new guy to stop, but it wasn't getting through. There was something wrong. Werewolves were trained to listen while in battle, so why wasn't he?

Faith faced him. "Bad, bad, doggie. You are in so much trouble. You should listen to Blake."

He growled and tried to punch her. "No way. I will get you for cutting me, I'm not a pansy who falls at a woman's feet."

She moved, blocked, and ducked as she slid under his legs on her knees, slashing what she could with the blade. His clawed hand grabbed her hair, pulling, while the other raked her back. She screamed again, and then a second later his clawed hand was removed by Bengie, who had a vise-like grip on the new guy's hand.

Just as Blake grabbed the new guy and spun him around they heard a loud howl followed by some other ones.

Faith winced. "Oh shit, new guy, you're dead now."

Blake sighed. "She's right. If you don't recognize her name I was using, how about the one her mate, the next in line to be alpha, calls her. Princess. I'm not a pansy either, but when a woman tells me she's the alpha's mate, I would definitely never hurt her. Contain her, yes."

The new guy changed back. His face turned pale and his body trembled. "I'm sorry, I don't know what came over me. I'm so sorry."

Blake snarled. "That's no excuse. You're two hundred years old, and you've been training since you were five. You should have known better."

There was a loud growl. Faith stumbled, her legs trembled then folded under her. Before she hit the ground, she felt strong hands catch her, lifting her. She glanced up at her brother, throwing her arms around him as he hugged her tight against him. She hugged him back. "Thanks, Bengie. I love you too."

Bengie smiled, showing sharp teeth. "I thought he was your mate, the big one. Mum said you would have a mate, she wouldn't tell me what that means exactly. She said I was too young, but I'm not, I'm a big boy, I just turned twelve."

A "holy shit" could be heard before she nodded and passed out.

* * * *

Kane was shocked. The princess he knew would never have done what she did. Four years ago his princess was a quiet, shy, little mouse. The last three days had really opened his eyes to a new woman. His princess was now a confident, stubborn, loyal—although she always had been, just more vocal—independent, feisty, alpha woman, ready to fight for what she wanted and believed right. Kane loved his old princess, but the new one was making him hotter than ever. Damn, he was so lucky. If at all possible he loved Faith more and more each day. He was sure if any other woman went through what she had gone through she would have cracked, but not his princess, she was the perfect woman to stand beside him, and someday help lead the pack.

Kane ran down to the cliffs, his brothers and father following. When they were in sight of the manhole they saw Faith being attacked by one of their wolves. He grabbed her by the waist, and Faith used a blade to slash and cut his hands, then she backflipped off him.

"Fuck, that was hot. She really did listen in practice."

Kane shot a glare at Jamie for that comment. But he did admit to himself she was a fantasy come to life. All she needed was tight leather pants and a fitted leather corset, and wham bam, she would be his walking wet dream. He shook his head.

Kane growled so loud he would swear the ground shook as the half-changed wolf tried to punch his Faith. She blocked and dived for his legs, slashing them.

The wolf was fucking dead for touching his princess. He picked up his speed and growled again when Blake grabbed the guy he now recognized as Luke. Luke was trembling and pale. Faith's body went limp, and the half-breed caught her just before she hit the ground.

A second later Kane reached them. "Give her to me." Bengie passed her over, and Kane studied her body, checking all her cuts and bruises, mentally calculating so he could treat any if necessary. To make sure Luke got the same done, he glanced over at his brothers and father. "You deal with that." He inclined his head toward Luke. "Because if I do it, I will kill him."

A dull, meaty thud and bones cracking reached Kane's hearing as he walked with his precious bundle back home, the half-breed following. His father growled, "Rules are rules, you touch a mate, and you pay the price. You're old enough to know we don't treat any woman like what you just did."

"Mum said she would be safe, but she's all bleeding, cut, and bruised. She is fighting people so they don't kill her. She's sad, I feel it." Bengie crossed his arms over his chest.

Reaching the back door, Kane turned to the half-breed and asked, "What do you mean she's sad?"

The half-breed's eyes furrowed and a look of concentration passed over his face. "She feels sad, and not just because her body hurts her."

Kane shook his head. "How the hell do you know, half-breed?"

"Mum had been trying to teach me. She said I could feel feelings inside people. I got it from her." He shrugged his big shoulders.

Kane kissed Faith and cuddled her closer to his body. She snuggled into his arms, sighed, and opened her beautiful brown eyes. She smiled at him and kissed his chest. Then, as if she remembered everything, she froze and sat up in his arms. Looking around, she yelled for Bengie.

"I'm here. He took you from me but I followed. I won't let anyone hurt you again. Sorry I got kind of scared before."

Faith smiled at him. "Oh, Bengie, I'm so sorry for these idiots. They will never hurt you again, will they, Dr. Wolfen?"

She glared daggers at him. He winced at the *Dr. Wolfen*. She only seemed to call him that when she was really pissed. Fuck, he had only just got back into her good books, she had been calling him Kane. She kept glaring at him, and he sighed and looked at the half-breed.

"You're welcome in our home."

Faith frowned. "And…"

"Maybe I shouldn't have put you in the hole."

Faith continued to frown. "And…"

Jeez, what else! He was not going to apologize for protecting her.

Faith did her own little growl at him, which made his dick stand to attention. Fuck, she was hot, even sitting in his arms battered, cut up, and bruised. He shook those thoughts out of his head and glared back at her.

"And I'm so..." He knew he was being childish by refusing to apologize, but he'd been protecting her.

She pulled his head down, whispering so softly that if he didn't have werewolf hearing he wouldn't have heard. "Say you're sorry to my brother, who is only twelve. If you don't, I'm sure one of your brothers would gladly give up a room or two for us."

He growled, frowned, and shook his head. Turning to the half-breed he whispered, "I'm sorry."

He could hear his brothers laughing at him.

Faith smiled. "I didn't hear that, Kane. Did you, Bengie?"

Bengie nodded and started to say yes, but Kane growled and nipped Faith's shoulder. "Don't push it, princess. That's the best you're going to get."

Faith smiled at him, and it was one of her smiles that brought the whole sun out. He opened the door to their house and everyone went inside.

Chapter 7

Faith was exhausted, both physically and mentally. The last four days had felt like a lifetime. She had learned Kane loved her. The man she had loved since she was a little girl. She had thought nothing would ever come of it since she was human and she believed he saw her as nothing more than a necessary evil. But now they were mated. Not only that, she had learned she was switched at birth and her biological mother taken by demons, where terrible things were done to her. She had a brother who was half-demon, she had fought a demon, helped save two special girls, and lastly she had the two most in-depth, longest, scariest visions of epic proportions that she'd ever had.

Kane sat on his ugly rocker armchair, and she was still in his arms. Bengie sat on the lounge, Griffen on the other end. Jamie and Jack sat in armchairs that matched the lounge. Eight chairs were scattered around the lounge room. Five were occupied by family members, and the other three contained Tray, their head pack enforcer, and two elders.

"Who has the girls?" Faith asked.

"They've been staying with us," Jack replied. "We thought it best. They get on so well with Ava and Eve, and they just loved Emma and Josie."

Faith smiled at Jack. "I'm sorry about before, but I didn't want to be stopped."

He smiled. "Werewolf healing." Then he frowned. "How are your new cuts?"

She winced but was starting to feel better. "Thanks to mating a werewolf, I have advanced healing, and once I have a shower, they won't be as bad as the demons' were."

She felt Kane wince. He kissed her mouth gently.

Faith smiled up at him. "Do you know how much I love you?" She wiggled her toes and pouted, pointing to her feet. He shook his head so she played dirty, she pouted her lips and stared into his eyes. "Please, they wouldn't be like this if somebody had treated my baby brother better."

He growled, "Jamie, go and get the foot cream out of the bathroom."

Jamie got up. Faith added, "Jamie, just get the vanilla scented one from my bag."

He nodded and left the room. When he returned with the cream Kane started massaging her feet as everyone quieted down and waited to be told the important new information that had been learnt.

"You know I'm only doing this because I love you, right?"

She frowned at Kane. "I don't know how loved I'm going to be after all the information I have to tell everyone."

* * * *

Faith just wanted to curl into a ball and sleep for a week. When everyone left, it was late. Afternoon lunch and dinner had been consumed. The visions were talked about, the girls were discussed, the demons and tunnels were talked about, and so was Bengie. Faith explained they needed to find supernatural people before the demons. Jack had spoken to several other alphas. All were grateful for the information, but only two had had similar problems. They had confirmed their greatest fears. So during the week they would talk to all the other alphas.

No definite decisions had been made other than what was going to happen to the girls. Della and Jack had fallen in love with them, and so had the rest of the family, so they were going to adopt them if the girls were okay with it. Faith and Kane were asked first, but with everything going on and them having Ben, Faith knew it was best for Jack and Della to take the girls.

They set Bengie up in the bedroom two rooms down from their room, next to the main bathroom, and showed him how to work the small TV and DVD player. Kane even set up his old PlayStation, which like any teenager or child,

Bengie loved. They then left the room so he could play. Faith walked out of the room telling Bengie they would have to try venturing to the shops because he needed clothes. Distracted by the video game, he simply nodded.

Faith finally showered, telling Kane no when he tried to join her. Lying on the bed, Kane snuggling her, she slowly relaxed.

"Tomorrow is the last day I could get off, princess, so I want to spend most of the day, if possible, just you and me. Once I'm back at work you will have a chance to get to know your brother."

Faith sighed. "I know we have to talk about you going back to work and me looking for a job."

"Faith, you don't need to get—"

"Nuh-uh, no talking. I just want to cuddle for five or ten minutes before we have to talk."

He sighed and pulled her closer. Faith reached up and kissed his neck then snuggled into him, falling asleep.

* * * *

Kane awoke to his princess kissing, licking, and sucking her way down his body, where she found what she seemed to be looking for. She blew on his dick before sucking as much of his cock in her mouth as she could, then she swirled her tongue around it. He growled as she moved her hands up his chest and then scratched down.

"Please tell me this isn't a dream."

A *pop* sounded as she let go of his cock, and she smiled up at him. "Not unless you want it to be."

He grunted and grabbed her waist, swapping positions so she was on the bottom. "Where's your brother?" he asked. "I can't hear him."

He looked down at the most succulent pair of breasts he'd ever seen. He let out a deep, satisfied growl as he sucked on one of the pointed, pink nipples, filling his mouth with her chocolate-vanilla taste.

"Ahhhh, Kane...ah, ah, my favorite brother of yours, Arden, has taken Bengie out for the...day to...ahhhh." She arched as he put a finger in her wet pussy.

"God, you're already wet," he groaned out.

She moaned again as he added a second finger, then he moved down her body and sucked her clit as he moved his fingers in and out. His tongue lapped at her pussy. He removed his fingers before she orgasmed.

"Kane… Please, I needed..."

"No, you're going to come around my dick as you ride me hard."

He flipped them so she was on top. Fuck, she looked hot. Her long, brown-red hair was wild, her eyes were hooded, her cheeks pink, her usually small top lip full and puffy, and she had a wicked smile on her face.

"So how do you want to spend the day? I suppose we should stop so we can talk about it."

He growled. "Talk is overrated."

He lifted her body and slid his dick home in her welcome heat. She threw her head back, and the look of pure pleasure on her face as she helped him slip her down on his cock was priceless. He had never seen a face look so utterly captivating.

Faith's tight pussy muscles clenched around him. God, this was heaven, he didn't want it to ever end. She leaned forward, kissing him. Scorching hot heat ran through his veins. That happened every time Faith touched him, but today there was something wild about her, like she couldn't get enough of him.

He breathed in the air and noticed that her chocolate-vanilla smell was stronger than usual, it was making him crazy. She growled and bit him hard. His wolf went crazy, and he growled back, sitting up, but she shoved him back down with a strength females only had when in heat.

Kane fought his wolf for control as he looked up into his princess's bright brown eyes. He knew if they kept going she would end up pregnant. He looked at her stomach, imagining it round with his child. God, he so wanted that. She would be the best mother. He grinned, maybe it would slow her down, make her be more careful.

He breathed in the intoxicating smell again, and this time his wolf won. He flipped a snarling, fighting Faith onto her hands and knees, draping himself over her and plunging his cock back into her welcoming depths, moaning at the extra tightness. She bucked and pushed against him, which made his wolf fight for dominance.

She laughed a husky sound. "Come on, Kane, harder."

He growled, pulling almost all the way out, then slammed home.

"Kane, more!" she screamed.

He obliged and started sucking her neck. She moved to turn around and he bit down on her shoulder over her mate mark. She yelled his name as she came around his cock, squeezing the life out of it. He couldn't hold it in, he came like he had never come before in his life. The base of his cock swelled so much he thought it would burst.

She moaned. "God, I loved that."

He moved them to the side, cuddling her close, his cum continuing to squirt inside her. He wondered if he should tell her what happened, that thanks to mating him she had gained some werewolf traits, had gained a lot more than he thought, one being going into heat. For their kind this happened to their women every six months but could be brought on earlier by finding a mate, and obviously, that also applied to human mates.

Kane breathed in her scent. God, her chocolate-vanilla smell was still so strong. He growled and nipped her neck. She shivered, grounding her bottom down, but it didn't move much as he was still locked inside her. He sucked on her neck and gently nipped her ear. One of his hands moved around to play with her clit and the other caressed her nipples.

"Kaaaannee."

He smiled as she moaned out his name. "Did I tell you how much I love your breasts? They're better than anything I could imagine." He moved his hand from her clit to the other breast. "They're so full, soft, more than a handful."

He slid one of his hands over her stomach, which he knew by the end of the day would grow with his child. He touched her belly ring. "When did you get this?"

She gave a sultry laugh. "I have seen you eyeing it. You've been dying to ask, haven't you?"

She laughed again, and he growled and nipped her neck.

"All right, I'll tell you. It was a present. Remy and I

got it done for our eighteenth birthdays. Well, I waited a month until she was eighteen, and then we went together. Sara didn't want one. She started going into all that stuff about what could happen if they did it wrong or if it got infected, blah, blah, blah. I swear she's a forty-year-old stuck in a twenty-year-old body. If it wasn't for Remy and me, she would act like a stuffy old lady. My God, the stuff she says." She shook her head and grinned. "You know, stuff you would have probably said."

He pinched her nipple and nipped her shoulder. She moaned out a laugh.

"So you think I'm stuffy and old? Ha! I'll show you, us old guys have the best stamina."

Chapter 8

Kane awoke to Arden yelling, "I'm back. Done with all my babysitting, so stop your fun. Mum and Dad said they could hear you from their house."

Faith pulled the cover over her head and whispered, "Please tell me he's joking."

Kane chuckled and kissed her forehead. "Yes, I think."

She smacked him on the chest.

Kane tickled her, pulling the covers off. "Come on, princess, the real world calls."

She crawled out of bed, pulling jeans and a singlet on. He shoved on jeans of his own, then picked her up and took her to the kitchen where he sat her down next to her brother who started talking before he even let his hand fall away.

"Hey sis, Arden took me to the shops. I got lots of things. He said it was better if I went with him so I didn't get stuck with you two lovebirds."

Faith smiled, walked over, and kissed Arden's cheek. "Thanks for taking him. I love you for it."

Kane growled. "Hey, no kissing anyone but me."

"I'm starving. What are we going to do for dinner? I would cook, but there's nothing in the fridge or cupboards until I shop." Faith glared at Kane whilst she said that.

Arden came to his rescue. "Well, you're going to love me even more because amongst all that, I bought Indian food."

She kissed Arden's cheek again. "Oh, you're so right, I love you a thousand times more now."

She sorted through the bags until she found what she was looking for. "Dish me out some while I put all Bengie's new stuff in the washing machine. Come on, Bengie, tell me all about your day while they heat and dish out."

As soon as she was out of hearing distance Arden asked, "Did you get to talk to Faith? I gave you plenty of time to talk, not do the nasty the whole time."

"We talked."

Arden raised his eyebrow.

"Well, I was going to talk, but she attacked me this morning."

Arden raised his eyebrow again.

"What! Don't look at me like that." Memories of earlier assaulted him as he groaned. "She did attack me. I tried to fight her, but she's evil."

Arden laughed. "You're a grown man who's scared to talk to his five foot nothing woman. You're a doctor for Christ's sake. What do you do at work when one of the nurses come up to you batting her eyelashes and pouts to get you to do something?"

Kane ran his fingers through his hair and sighed. "Trust me, if she only did that maybe I could have resisted her, but with her in heat and her being my mate I..."

"She's in what?"

Kane swore. Fuck, he hadn't wanted Arden to know. "Yeah, she went into heat, but don't say anything yet. I haven't had a chance to tell her. I don't know how she will react and…"

Faith walked back into hearing distance. Kane glanced at Arden, silently pleading for him to keep quiet. His brother gave a slight nod as an answer. Thinking he was in the clear, at least for now, Kane relaxed.

Halfway through dinner Arden asked, "Faith, what are you going to do about your friend coming to see you in what…five days?"

Faith choked on her food. "Shit, with everything that's been going on I forgot. We're just good friends. I'm sure when I tell him what has happened he'll understand. I'm not the only reason he's coming." Kane was ready to rip the guy apart, so he almost missed when Faith whispered softly, "It's not like we had sex or anything."

This time Arden choked on his food.

Kane smiled until Bengie piped up. "Arden said you have to go back to work. Who's going to take care of Faith then?"

Kane was about to answer when Faith glared at him.

"I can take care of you and myself. I don't need a babysitter." She rolled her eyes as she said the last bit. "Don't worry, Bengie, I'm going to be busy tomorrow looking for a job and practicing controlling my visions."

Kane tried not to frown. He didn't like her holding off her visions. He knew for a fact she got bad migraines when she tried to do that. He forced a smile. "Princess, you don't have to hold off your visions. I know that gives you migraines. And I earn plenty of money. Why don't you just stay home and help the pack?"

"I love my job, and I want to work."

"I prefer that you didn't. Actually, I insist you not work right now. It's too dangerous, and it's not necessary."

Arden groaned, deliberately kicking Kane under the table, but it was too late. Faith gave him a death stare.

"I can do what, Dr. Wolfen? Stay home, be a good little mate, help the pack, live off your plenty of money, *really*." The last word was screeched.

Arden stood up quickly. "Hey Ben, how about we go show my mum all we got today? She was asking me to bring you round."

Bengie didn't get a chance to respond before Arden dragged him out of the house.

As soon as they were out of the door Faith turned on Kane and glared at him.

"So, Kane, is that what you want in a mate? Is that what you think you need, what you think I need, or are you just making a suggestion?"

Fuck, what was he supposed to say? "The other women I've been with just wanted to stay at home, spend money, go out to fundraisers, and have fancy parties."

Faith gaped opened-mouthed at him by the time he ended. She pulled herself up straight to her full height of five foot three, shut her mouth, turned, and started to walk away.

"Why are you walking away?"

She whirled around, her fists clenched, giving Kane a look that if looks could kill he would be dead.

"I didn't realize I'm one of your 'other women'. I really thought you knew a little bit about me. I may not have spoken to you in four years, but for ten years you were in my life, you would save me from the dragon, get Jamie and Devlin to scare the boys who picked on me, you let me cry on your shoulder, you knew most of my secrets. For

Christ's sake, you even let me trick you into being my dance partner for ballroom dancing. My God, even in the four years we didn't talk I know you asked about me. Sometimes I felt, knew, you were outside the front door, listening. Waiting, knowing I would leave as soon as you came in. Now all of a sudden you don't know me at all. No wonder I left the frigging country to get over you. Well, that's how it started out. Then I started to enjoy myself, my independence, I guess that's why I stayed so long. The last two months before I came home I was having fewer visions. I had heard you were with a woman and it was serious. There was even talk you were going to mate her, so I thought it was safe to come home." She smiled a bitter smile. "Stupid me, I haven't even asked where this woman is that your brothers talked about. You would think with me being a psychic I would know, but no, anything to do with you I rarely got a glimpse or feeling of."

Kane winced. He debated whether he should tell her everything. "We lied, made her up. We all thought if you thought I was settled, distracted with a mate, you would come home. Everyone started to worry when you started dating." He growled. "Then you started talking about Brett."

"Brad," Faith corrected.

"How you really liked him, that there could be something between you and him, so that's when my brothers told you I was going to mate the woman. You booked your flight home right after you were told that."

He looked down at her now. Tears streamed down her face, and he used his thumb to wipe them away.

"I could never have another mate because there has always, is always going to be you. I'm so sorry we deceived you, but we…*I* needed you home with me. I couldn't stand the emptiness anymore. I missed when you would call me just to tell me what one of my goofball brothers had done or what you had done that day." He moved her over to the lounge and placed her on his lap. "Do you know my brothers stopped calling me when they figured out I was the reason you weren't coming home? Please don't be angry, you don't have to come to the parties or functions. I love you, I want you to be happy." Kane kissed her lips lightly, hugging her close.

* * * *

Faith couldn't believe all she had just been told. She should be angry that they had tricked her into coming home, but how could she be anything but filled with love after that confession?

"I don't mind going to some parties or fundraisers. I

love you. I want you to be happy too. I'm not thrilled you all tricked me, but I know it was done with good intentions."

They sat for a while just hugging, snuggling, and talking about old times.

Bengie came in later yelling, "Arden's in the car. He said Jamie's going to come around tomorrow to play video games with me and help you find a job." He stopped yelling when he came upon them. He smiled. "I got a new game, Star Wars." He ran to his room saying, "I'm going to go play it."

Kane kissed her. "He's so big I'm scared to think what's going to happen when he hits puberty."

Faith laughed.

* * * *

The next morning came way too early. At six o'clock the alarm went off, and Faith groaned. "Noooo, don't take away my heater, the best pillow ever."

Kane chuckled. "I'm glad to know I'm needed for something."

Faith snuggled into his chest.

"Princess, I would love to spend another day with you, but we're swamped at work. I already had five days off, people pulling doubles for me, I'm going to owe some favors."

Faith groaned again, clinging to him harder for a second. "Go." She clung to him a moment or two longer, then reluctantly let him go.

Kane kissed her lips. "I love waking up to you on top of me. I think I found my little piece of heaven."

Faith smiled and pushed Kane away. "Go to work."

Faith fell back to sleep and woke a couple of hours later to loud whispers.

"She's had a busy couple of days, let her sleep."

"But she wanted to be up early so she could call about jobs."

Faith put the pillow over her face, moaning. She pulled it off and yelled, "I'm up. Give me ten to fifteen minutes."

Twenty-five minutes later, she was ringing around for a job and faxing resumes. She practiced calling up a vision then later calling up one and holding it off. By late afternoon she had a job at the after school care she'd worked at for six months before she left the country. They wanted her to start tomorrow. Faith was so excited about getting a job she went out to get groceries so she could cook a celebration dinner—roast chicken, baked potatoes, sweet potatoes, corn, and pumpkin. She was even going to make a chocolate cake.

Jamie came in as she was putting the chicken in the oven.

"Are we celebrating something?"

"Several things, actually, like Kane and I becoming mates, me having a brother, and me getting a job."

Jamie grinned. "That's great, but I still think I would have made a better mate for you."

Faith smiled. "You know I love you, Jamie, but I'm not in love with you. That kiss we had was nice but nothing sparked. Trust me, you're going to love your mate, all my werewolves are."

Jamie stared at her as she walked away.

* * * *

Kane loved his job, but today had felt like a whole week of days rolled into one. He couldn't wait to get home to Faith. He'd had to take off his watch so he stopped counting down the hour, minutes, and seconds before he could go home. He'd even turned down a double shift, which he never did. His work mates were shocked, but Kane was determined to be home by six o'clock at the latest. As he was getting ready to leave a close friend and colleague, Dr. Jerome Stark, came up behind him.

"I just heard the funniest thing—you're not pulling a double. Are you sick?" He made a show of touching Kane's forehead.

Kane chuckled. "No, I just want to get home."

Jerome's brows furrowed as he shook his head. "The nurses said you've been acting weird. What's up? You hate going home. To quote what you said last week, 'to a big, empty house'."

Kane grinned. "It's not empty anymore."

Jerome sighed. "Please don't tell me you sold that ginormous, beautiful house, because I know for a fact you built that house for someone you call princess."

Kane frowned, he didn't know he had mentioned Faith. "I said that?"

"A couple of times, although after saying it you shook your head and corrected yourself by saying you'd built it for your future wife."

Kane was shocked. "Oh, I didn't sell it. My princess is in it. I mat...married her."

Jerome nodded, then yelled when the last of what he'd said sunk in. "What! You married the princess, the one you're always talking about?"

Kane suppressed a growl at Jerome. "I do not always talk about her. In fact, I didn't even know I did talk about her."

Jerome laughed. "Well, you do. It's odd, I don't even

think you realize you're doing it."

"She came back from overseas. I kind of didn't give her a chance to say no to me."

Jerome smiled. "Go home, I'll cover you if they need you for anything."

"Thanks, buddy. I owe you one."

"Yeah, yeah. You know, one of these days I'm going to find out her real name."

Kane laughed as he headed for his car.

* * * *

As soon as Kane opened his car door, the sweet aroma of a roast dinner hit him. He rushed inside to find Jamie and Bengie playing video games. He walked to the kitchen to see the most delectable sight—Faith's lush arse sticking out of the oven as she turned potatoes and added garlic bread.

Without saying a word, she shut the oven, turned, and jumped up on him, wrapping her legs around him. She bit his earlobe and whispered, "You're early."

He groaned as she sealed her lips over his. Her hands came up to tug on his hair, and he moved his hands down to cup her arse, kneading it. Faith moaned into his mouth, kissing him like she hadn't seen him in days. They broke away, panting, when the oven timer went off.

She whispered in his ear what she had on underneath

her clothes. "I have a matching black lace set on. Wanna guess if it's got bows?"

He growled through clenched teeth as she moved away from his arms back to the oven.

"Well, so much for that hot shower I've been looking forward to all day. Now I will be having a cold shower."

She giggled at him.

* * * *

After dinner Kane finally got rid of Jamie, shoving him outside with a piece of cake. Jamie laughed, saying he would be back tomorrow. When Kane came back in Faith was sitting on the lounge reading a book. He picked her up, sitting her on his lap. She placed her book on the coffee table and snuggled into him. Kane hugged her closer, trying to say what he had to say carefully.

"You start work tomorrow. I know you want to work. I have no problem with it, but I am glad it's only part time."

She glared at him.

"Before you get angry, all I'm saying is I think it would be best for you as you have been getting visions." He held up his hand so he could finish. "I know you can look after yourself, but I'll still worry."

She kissed him slowly before saying, "It should be fine. It's only at the after school program, which is ages six and up."

"Just don't overdo it."

Faith nodded.

He debated if he should tell her what he had been thinking of doing as he hadn't fully decided himself yet. Hugging her tighter to him, he blurted out, "I'm thinking I might stop working at the hospital and become a local doctor, maybe not even full time, join a clinic three to four days a week."

* * * *

Faith was shocked. She knew Kane loved working in the fast pace of the emergency room.

"But you love your job."

"I did before I had you. One of the reasons I loved that job so much was because I thought it kept me so busy I didn't even think about you, but today I was told I talked about you quite a bit. I hated coming home to this empty house, but tonight I couldn't get away from the hospital fast enough. I had to take off my watch to stop checking the time."

He moved her so her legs straddled him. Faith stared into his eyes and chewed on her bottom lip, trying to decide how to word what she wanted to say. "I don't want to be the reason you resign from your job. If it makes you happy, I'm sure we can figure something out, like cutting back on your hours or maybe—"

Kane captured her mouth before she could continue. He groaned against her lips, and she slid her hands up and under his shirt, hugging him to her. Kane gently gathered her hands, moving them behind her before he ended their kiss and eased down her body, worshipping her. When he reached her belly button he paused and looked up at her as he said, "Bengie asleep?" He placed feathered kisses on her stomach, which sent butterflies coursing through her. She groaned when he stopped to add, "What do you want to do?"

Faith smiled at him as she sighed. "Oh, I don't know. What do you have in mind?"

He tugged her singlet off, pulling the black lace bra down and sucking a nipple into his mouth.

"Oh, oh, Kaannnee."

He chuckled. "Might want to quiet down, princess. We wouldn't want to wake your brother."

She bit the inside of her check as she nodded.

His hands slowly moved back to her stomach, catching her pants and pulling them off.

He looked at her. "God, you're beautiful."

Faith felt her checks heat, blushing as he buried his

face in between her legs, feasting. He chuckled against her pussy and she shivered. The smell of her arousal intensified. He licked the cream from her pussy until she felt the tremors of a pending orgasm. He moved up her body, thrusting his dick home. She came, calling his name, the word muffled against his shoulder. He thrust several more times. His face was strained and his muscles seemed to tighten as her vagina muscles squeezed and released.

Kane turned her over, placing her hands on the lounge and spreading her legs further apart. She turned her head to see him take a step back, looking at her in an erotic stance. Growling, he stepped forward, draping himself over her and kissing his way up her back as he slammed his cock back home.

* * * *

Kane slowly moved his hands up, stopping at her stomach, knowing his child grew safely inside her. He cupped her breasts, playing with the nipples, loving her reactions. She writhed and bucked back against him, moaning his name. He picked up his pace, moving a hand up to help steady her.

"Harder, please, harder. I need..." She bit his hand, and he growled, moving faster. She chanted, "Yes, yes, yes."

Stroking her clit with one hand, he braced her with the

other as he thrust into her with more force. She screamed her release, obviously not caring anymore about waking up her brother. Her pussy clenched so tightly around his cock he couldn't hold out any longer, and he came, yelling his own release as his cock locked inside her. God, it felt so good. He felt Faith shiver against him. She moaned as he picked her up and carried her to their room. Each time he moved, her body seemed to vibrate against him and her vagina muscles squeezed until it felt like she was going to cut his cock off.

As he laid them on the bed, spooning and cuddling, she spoke softly in a blissed-out voice. "Once you go wolf, you will never want to go back. I love my werewolf."

He chuckled and kissed her head. Faith pulled his hand up to her mouth and kissed it. "I love you, Kane."

He pulled her closer and sucked on her neck. "You feel so good, my princess. I'm going to take you slowly this time…kissing, licking, sucking, and savoring every inch, finding all the special places on your body. By the end of tonight I will know every inch of you by heart."

She sighed out her pleasure as he did just that.

* * * *

The damn alarm went off, although it felt like they'd only fallen asleep minutes earlier. She groaned, snuggling closer to Kane. "I love you, Kane. Don't forget I start work today. I finish tonight at 7:30, but I won't get home 'til about 8:20, so there's no need for you to rush home. I know you're a workaholic. From what I was told you usually didn't get home until around 10:30 at night, and then you would go out patrolling for two to three hours."

He chuckled. "Seems like I'm not the only one who listens to information about the other."

Faith smiled and pushed him out of bed. "Go to work."

He chuckled again.

Faith had a slow morning before she went to work. She spent time with Bengie, relaxed, and after lunch she left for work.

It felt fantastic to be home in Australia, working, coming home to Kane and Bengie. Faith had two wonderful vision free days where she got to sleep in, go to the beach, and she even did some shopping. On the third day, about an hour and a half before she finished work, her peaceful days came to an end. She almost missed catching the vision to hold it, because she was busy helping a group of girls with their artwork. She excused herself to go to the bathroom so she could gather herself, and she stared at her reflection in the mirror, concentrating. This was the first vision she'd had to hold off since getting her extra power. Faith cursed her mother for the gift. She could feel how powerful the vision was going to be. All Faith's senses were on alert. She rinsed her face and walked back out.

At 7:38 PM, Faith was walking out the door to go home. She thanked her coworker for staying back to help her pack up and lock everything up, then hurried to her car and broke all the speed limits getting to the house. Pulling into the driveway, she honked the horn, which didn't help her migraine. She waited for Kane to come out, but Jamie strolled out instead. She saw him smile her way, then he frowned and started running when he saw her face.

She finally let the vision come.

> *Faith was in the city in back of a place similar to Splash, except more like a bar. She looked around the back alley and saw two large doors, one a fire exit. Across from her were cars, bins, and the doors of another establishment. She knew it was late, around 11:30 PM to 12ish.*
>
> *Five women dressed in black uniforms came out laughing.*
>
> *"I can't believe you put up with that grabbing, Lexie. I would have poured his*

drink over him. The arsehole, just because he's the owner's brother doesn't excuse it."

The one called Lexie laughed. "I know, but he's so cute."

All the girls laughed harder. A small, blonde, pixie-like woman spoke up this time. "My God, he's only eighteen now, just think what he'll be like in his eighties. He'll definitely give the phrase 'dirty old man' a new meaning."

They laughed harder, then the one called Lexie and a tall, black-haired woman with green eyes turned pale. They looked at each other then said together, "We need to leave now. Come on, quick, to our cars."

They grabbed the three other women and started running down the alley, where Faith saw a small parking area of about fifteen to twenty cars. The three women asked Lexie and Stacy to stop scaring them, but the women ignored their companions. They didn't make it halfway before they were surrounded by three huge demons and about fifteen minions.

One of the demons stepped forward. "We only want you two." He pointed to Lexie and Stacy then turned to the minions. "You may kill and feed on the others."

They attacked as the girls screamed.

Faith came out of the vision with a splitting migraine, a sense of direction, and a rough estimate of how long they had. She yelled, not realizing she was in Jaime's arms on the lounge.

"Call your father, Jamie. We have to go ASAP. Please, call now. I don't have time to explain everything twice. Tell him we'll need back-up."

Five minutes later Jack, Rane, Blake, Devlin, and a human major named Samuel Black arrived. Faith stared at the major then turned to Rane.

"No offense to the major over there, but why the hell is he here? Rane, I thought you handled all military? Aren't you in charge anymore?"

"No offense taken," the major said even as he scowled at her.

She stared at them until Rane sighed and ran his hands over his head. "The humans have decided they need to see how bad it is, what it takes to fight them. It's getting so bad, and we can't be everywhere. They're seeing the ramification, so they want to help. Plus, the number of missing people in the last five years has tripled, so they want to help find them. They sent Major Black to see what we're up against. I think we're going to need the help if what you've told us you saw is coming, and from what's been happening lately on our nightly watches, I feel you're right."

Faith sighed. "Well, we could use him for this one because there are three non-supernaturals, and if we need to go to the hospital his clearance could come in handy." Faith told them about the vision, explaining that she knew the direction and had a feeling of where to go and a rough time. "I'll go with you and feel my way like I did before. This time I have a better sense of when everything is going to happen."

The five werewolves said, "No! You're not coming."

She glared at them all. "You have no choice. All your patrols are out, you even have your spares out, there are five women who are going to need someone to help them. I have the weapons and I trained with you all. You're taking him!" She pointed at the major.

Jack shook his head. "No way, Faith. He's military

trained, seen battles before, been in them."

Faith smiled at Jack. "So have I. Or have you forgotten that the other night I helped take down a demon? Come on, Jack. I'll be really careful to stay away from the demons and only save the women, calm them, and help them. Come on, please. You have every available werewolf out there."

She tried not to smile as five men groaned in defeat.

"You have fifteen minutes to get ready," Jack said. "I'll stay here close to central, monitoring movement. Make sure you phone in any new information. Any teams close by that aren't busy I'll send to help. Faith, if anything happens to you I will throttle you personally."

Faith nodded at Jack before she rushed off to get ready.

Chapter 9

Faith was ready ten minutes later with fitted, black leather pants, a black singlet top, and a pink leather knife vest which she shook her head at because it pushed her assets up like an offering. It had been a present from Jamie on her eighteenth birthday that was meant as a joke, or so she thought. She came out of the room tying a band on her braid, to four slacked-jawed werewolves.

"Holy shit, and you said I suck at giving presents. All you need now is knee-high, fuck-me boots and a whip, then you're about every guys' walking wet dream."

Faith rolled her eyes at Jamie, smiling. "Lucky for me I have the shit-kickers Rane bought me for my eighteenth birthday. You guys really know how to buy a girl a present. To think you have four sisters." She shook her head.

Faith heard Jack chuckle before he turned to remind them not to hesitate to call. He grabbed her by the arm as they were leaving. "Remember, Faith, use the long knife as an extension of your body. It's a dance, and they're your dance partners that aren't allowed to touch you."

She nodded and ran after the boys.

Jack yelled, "Rane, don't forget that the major is your

responsibility."

They drove to the city in record time knowing they had roughly thirty minutes to find the place. They passed the nightclub district, heading for the restaurant and pub section. The sense of direction became stronger until Faith knew they were close. She told them to stop, and they all got out and started walking toward a pub called O'Malley's. Just before they reached the alley they heard screams and ran to get to the women. Two of the demons had hold of Lexie and Stacy. The other three women were screaming against the alley wall, huddled together and trying to battle off minions.

Faith pulled her long knives with their tips iced. She yelled, "The major and I will kill the minions."

The werewolves nodded, and Rane hesitated for a moment, glaring at her. She raised her eyebrow at him, daring him to say anything. He sighed and joined the others.

Faith turned to the major who looked like he was trying to mask his horrified expression. "Major, remember to cut the wings, then the heart and head."

He nodded, pulling out the knives Rane had given him.

They ran into the minions, the major on one side and Faith on the other. About half the minions turned to attack them. She tuned out the women's screams, focusing on the ugly creatures that flew over her head scratching and biting. She arched, stretching her arms up, then swung them down in an arch, slicing the wings and one minion's head. She spun and took a step forward, taking more wings. She then focused on stabbing the hearts. Faith whirled again, moving her arms in a circle, catching the last of the minions attacking her.

Faith swore as zombies came after her and the major. She swore again as she looked at the frozen look on the major's face, knowing that Rane had failed to tell him about zombies. As zombies were about to kill the major, Faith yelled, "Fuck, look out, major!"

He turned as she chopped a zombie's head off.

"They're not humans anymore. Look how white they are, their eyes are black, they only listen to their demon master, and they have inhuman strength. Focus, major!" she yelled as a minion and zombie attacked her. That seemed to get through to him as he attacked them with renewed strength.

Faith spun, slicing minions, only to smell smoky sulphur and be grabbed by a demon.

"You are the one we really want. I will get my reward for bringing you in."

Faith could feel his long talon nails sticking into her

head as he lifted her off the ground by her hair. She guessed him to be about twelve feet, so before he turned her to face him she calculated the distance to the ground. Praying, she screamed and turned, lifting her arm and slashing it behind her. He roared and it sounded like scratching nails on a chalkboard. Faith cut his hand off, flipping and landing hard on her feet to stand in front of the demon. She managed to avoid its spiked tail as he swung it at her, but his foot kicked her and she fell back, landing against the wall. She silently thanked Jamie for the specially made clothes and Rane for the shit-kickers.

Her hands burned from the demon's acid blood and her body ached. She looked up at the massive demon. His red skin glistened, his horns were long and sharp. He smiled down at her, showing his sharp, long, pointed teeth. Faith calmed herself, knowing she had to stall as she knew more minions and demons had arrived, keeping the four werewolves busy. Faith felt the major come slowly up beside her. She signaled for him to get behind the demon and mouthed *head*. The demon laughed, the grating noise making her shudder.

"Ahhh, I see you are getting desperate now, using ordinary humans." He laughed again. "They are nothing but food, slaves, and playthings, but don't worry, there won't be many left when we take over this planet. Our army will destroy most of them, pitiful things. The ones we do keep alive will become slaves, breeders, and cattle to us for food."

She ignored the horrible images flashing through her head, knowing the demon was telling her this in the hope that it would distract her. He cackled and lunged for Faith, batting the major with his tail. She danced out of his way, slashing his arms, which gave her a chance to get close to his back.

She yelled to the major as she cut his tail off. "Go to the front and try to stab the heart, but whatever you do don't look into his eyes, that's how they lure you in so they can bite you and drain your blood which turns you into a zombie under their control."

The demon roared in pain as Major Black gave her a nod to show he understood. She climbed up his back as quick as possible, slashing his hand as he tried to reach her. He bucked and shook, trying to get her off, but she clung on for life. She knew she only had a small amount of time to get out of the way before he died and dropped to the ground, crushing her. Brushing up against the alley wall, reaching his massive shoulders, she held her special knives and wrapped her arm around the demon's neck. He grabbed her arms, and just as she felt her body start to get squished up against the wall she used all her strength to bring her knife hand toward her.

"Heart, now," Faith screamed at the major.

She knew he complied as the head rolled forward and the body fell against her. Using the wall, she leaned back and kicked her feet out, jumping off before he fell back again.

Finally running over to the three crying and terrified women huddled together, she looked down at them. She really needed them to cooperate before more demons or minions arrived. Looking into each of their eyes Faith told them, "Stop now! No more crying. Pull yourselves together or you will die. I need your cooperation to get out of here." She made sure she looked at each of them. "Get up now, follow me, do not run away, do not touch anything. Got it? All you have to do is follow me." She turned to one of the women and asked for her car keys. "I know you have a large car that we will all fit in."

The woman passed over her keys as they all got up nodding at her. They moved past Jamie and Devlin fighting two demons and four minions. Faith could see four demons' bodies near them.

One of the women behind her yelled out "Stacy" then

broke away, trying to reach her friend.

"Fuck," Faith swore. "You have to be joking. Now you decide you want to save your friend? Fucking idiot."

She turned, nodding to the major to take over, and grabbed the woman as one of the demon's tails slashed the side of her face.

"Shit!"

Faith sliced the tail off, pushing the woman out of the way. The minions turned to attack. Faith arched up on her toes, coming down, slicing wings then heads, knowing she had little time with the human woman's injures. She decided to help her boys. Running, jumping on the demon they fought, she cut the tail off. She didn't hesitate this time as she climbed up and wrapped her hands around his neck, slicing it off. She jumped off, bracing for the fall, and grabbed the woman, running after the major and the other two screaming women he was dragging to the car.

Faith scanned the area for Rane and Blake. Her heart fell when she saw ten minions, four demons, and six dead demons scattered about. She knew they couldn't last much longer, as they looked barely able to stand with their broken bones, cuts, and bruises. Their werewolf healing couldn't keep up with all the demons and their attacks. Usually it was one demon to two werewolves, so they were greatly outnumbered. She debated what to do and sighed in relief when Jamie joined in.

Devlin came over to her with Stacy in his arms and placed the woman at her feet. "Guard her for a minute. Yell if you need help," Devlin said as he ran over to help the fight.

She nodded and knelt down to help Stacy and to check the woman she had saved.

The women cried, "Is she dead? Please, she can't be. Wake up, Stacy!"

Faith ignored the women, focusing on their surroundings. Dead demons and minions were scattered everywhere. She had never seen so many, other than in her Armageddon visions. Fuck, they really wanted these women. She grabbed the phone from her vest to call Jack.

"We need major clean up here, Jack. They sent a lot more then I saw in my vision. Get here quick, I don't know how much longer Rane and Blake will last. They're in bad shape." She gave their coordinates and hung up.

Jamie came over to her. He grabbed his phone, took a picture of her, then picked up Stacy. "Get the girls to the hospital. We're taking Stacy and Lexie back to base. Kane will see to them. The major will help you out."

She nodded, then frowned. "Jamie, you didn't just take

a picture of me, did you?"

He shrugged then grinned. "What? You look so hot right now. This is going on my wall."

She couldn't help it, she laughed as she grabbed the woman, dragging her to the car the major had started. Faith pushed her in the car, angry with the woman's silliness in going after her friend alone.

"Drive, major. She's losing a lot of blood from the cut on the cheek and other places. I know the other women aren't in much better condition either."

They drove to the hospital in silence.

* * * *

Half an hour and Kane was out of there. He had pulled a double shift, well almost a triple. He couldn't wait to get home to his princess just to breathe her scent in and hold her close. He sighed and looked up to find his friend Dr. Jerome Stark.

"Are you deliberately ignoring your pager?"

He glanced down at his flashing pager. "Sorry, long day. Do you know what this is about?"

His friend smiled. "Yeah, our wet dream just walked in."

Kane chuckled. "You paged me to tell me this!"

Jerome shook his head as they headed for the

emergency. "Four twenty-somethings just come in with a Major Samuel Black. Three of the four women are injured with what looks like bite marks with flesh missing, cuts, and bruises. The fourth woman is the one I want. She doesn't seem to be injured."

Kane started to feel uneasy. As they got closer to the emergency room his wolf began growling as his friend continued.

"She's wearing black boots, tight black leather pants, a pink vest, and I'm not joking, buddy, she looks like a leather-clad Lara Croft but her breasts are bigger and her ponytail is almost to her backside."

Kane was walking so fast now that his colleague almost had to run to keep up with him.

"They're in room ten as it's the biggest. Kane, you can look after any of the others, but my fantasy woman is mine to check. Those brown eyes..."

Kane could already smell her over the disinfectant hospital smell. He bit his tongue to control his growl as he entered the room. Jerome headed toward Faith. Kane growled, shoving him against the wall. Jerome's eyes rounded and he looked at him with a shocked expression.

"Consider this a warming, Jerome. Friend or not, stay away from my wife."

He let go of him and stepped back, turning his head when he heard Faith speak. "Oh shit, I'm in trouble."

He glanced around the room. Three women were lying on beds, and his mate was sitting on the one in the corner, a man standing beside her…Major Black, he assumed. Kane ignored everyone else, going straight to Faith, knowing he was being unprofessional but not caring.

"Princess, where is Jamie?"

She sighed. "Hi, honey. Don't worry, I'm fine."

He frowned at her.

"Fine, Jamie is heading home where I hoped you were because your medical skills could be used."

He cupped her face and kissed her gently. A cleared throat interrupted him. He glanced up to see Dr. Jerome, who stared at him like he was trying to figure out a puzzle.

"I've called Dunsty and Callum as this is too close to you, Kane."

Kane nodded at Jerome. Ignoring everyone else for a moment, he stared at Faith. Taking her hand, he pulled her off the bed and out of the room with the major following. Kane was furious.

"Why the hell are you here, Faith, out without protection?"

He didn't care what had happened, she was his mate,

the next alpha female. Everyone better be dead or he would kill them. She was fucking pregnant. He held his wince as he thought that, glad he was only ranting in his mind because he was the only one who knew beside Arden, and he would kill Arden if he had let her go out.

Jerome cleared his throat again behind him. Kane growled.

Faith sighed, and she stepped forward, holding her hand out. "Hi. If you didn't figure it out already, I'm Kane's ma...wife."

Jerome's smile was huge. "Ah, the famous princess. I'm Dr. Jerome Stark."

Jerome laughed as Faith turned a pretty pink.

"Can I ask what your name is? Kane has never said it, he always calls you princess."

Faith laughed at this. "Faith, Faith York."

Kane growled. "Faith Wolfen."

Jerome nodded and smiled. "Can I just take Kane away for a moment?"

She nodded, shooing him off. They walked over to the nurse and doctors station.

"You have a lot of explaining to do, Kane. They have a clearance one for the situation for the girls in emergency, there's a list of questions I'm not allowed to ask, not to mention the condition of the women. Shit, Kane, do you know what the hell is going on?"

Kane watched as six more military men came in.

"They're making everyone sign a confidentiality agreement. What the fuck is going on?"

Kane tuned his friend out as he watched his wife introduce herself to the new military men. She was so hot in what she was wearing. He smiled, thinking of all the fantasies he was going to get her to fulfill when they got home.

Jerome nudged him again, sighing. "Just go, Kane. I can see I'm not going to get an answer, and if I had a wife who looked like that I wouldn't even be here. Go take her home, because you're an idiot if you don't notice how most of the men in here are eyeing her."

Kane nodded, wiping the smile off his face as he knew his teeth had lengthened. "Thanks."

He went over to the group of military men to introduce himself. He already knew two from his days in the military. He excused himself and Faith.

"I'll take you home if you give me five to ten minutes to get my things."

She smiled up at him, looking exhausted. "Thanks, I'll call your dad to tell him not to send anyone then. Major

Black will be coming back with us."

He nodded and gently pulled her into his arms. He leaned down, kissing the top of her head. As he glanced back up again, he groaned. *Ah, not tonight.* The woman just wouldn't give up. "I'm sorry, princess."

She glanced up at him, confused. "What are you sorry about?"

He turned her around, leaning down to whisper in her ear. "For what's about to descend on us. Dr. Bethany Balanco."

"Dr. Wolfen, I have a patient I want you to meet," Dr. Balanco purred out.

He gripped Faith tighter, shuddering in revulsion. It wasn't that the woman wasn't pretty, it was that she never gave up. No matter what he said, she threw herself at him every chance she got.

She ignored Faith, continuing on, "I was wondering if you—"

Her fingers crawled up his arm, he removed her hand. "Dr. Balanco, Dr. Stark will have to take it as I'm heading home with my wife."

She looked startled for a moment then finally noticed Faith. "We didn't know Kane was married," she said to Faith. "He's never mentioned you. I hope you know how disappointed all the ladies will be. Kane was thought to be one of our most eligible bachelors, and we have all wanted to get our hands on him."

He felt Faith straighten against him. "We've only been married a couple of days, but I've been a family friend for years. I just returned from overseas, and Kane grabbed me and hasn't let me go. So all the other women will have to find a new bachelor to hang off, because this one belongs to me." Faith held out her hand. "Well, it was a pleasure to meet one of Kane's colleagues, but if you'll excuse me, I need to go help my colleague make something disappear." Faith dropped her hand when Dr. Balanco glanced at her outstretched hand then ignored it.

Giving a shrug at the woman's rudeness, Faith turned and her lips met Kane's. She nipped his top lip as her tongue traced his bottom lip. He moaned, forgetting where he was and who was around. Kane held her tight, not wanting to let go.

Faith ended the kiss, whispering, "I love you."

She then went over to talk to Major Black and his companions. Kane bit his cheek to stop himself from laughing at the horrified expression on Dr. Balanco's face as Faith made a dramatic head gesture her way. Dr. Balanco didn't even say bye when she left.

Kane walked to his office with a huge smile on his face.

* * * *

Faith walked out of the hospital with Major Black beside her.

"I called Jack to let him know Kane is going to take us home. I think it's probably good for you to get to know Kane better since he'll be the head alpha when Jack retires." She sat down on the seat in front of the hospital. She leaned her head against the back with more force that she'd intended and she winced, then sighed as all the adrenaline went out of her. She looked up at the major's concerned face. "I never wanted this." She whispered, but he caught it.

"I'm assuming he wasn't supposed to be there."

Faith shook her head. "Fuck." She banged her head back. "Would you believe me if I told you I wanted to be normal?"

He smiled at her. "I thought you were their sister as you fight like a werewolf. I didn't know you were human and related by marriage."

She closed her eyes, fighting the exhaustion. "I'm human, well, psychic, supernatural. I grew up with them, that's how I learned to fight." She opened her eyes and stood up, looking across the grass area. "I've just returned from two years overseas away from all this. I needed to find myself. I wanted to be normal, I had to get away." She wrapped her arms around herself. "I came back from overseas and straightaway I'm thrown back into all this, and mated to Kane, who I love with all my heart. I would gladly go through anything just to be with him. I loved him from the first moment I laid eyes on him, but being thrown back into it all..." She sighed. "My visions before I left were never this strong, long, or thorough. I'm really just trying to figure out my place in all this."

She looked up at him before turning away because she didn't want to see his reaction to her selfishness. "I'll tell you a secret, when I was overseas I stayed away from everything paranormal. I even held off my visions until I had them so rarely I actually felt normal for a while. I didn't want all off this." She pointed to the hospital then herself in her leather getup. "I wasn't going to be special, psychic, odd, weird, or strange. I was going to be a normal-with-no-paranormal-in-my-life woman. At least I got to try it. I knew they had weres check on me, but for a little time I got to live like a normal nineteen to twenty year old single woman."

Faith laughed a hollow sound. "Do you know I'll be twenty-one in a couple of months? I sure do feel a lot older." She shook her head as tears slid down her cheeks and she wiped them away. "Don't get me wrong, I love all my werewolves, but they always kind of smothered me. I could never tell them what I've just told you, they would freak out."

She finished her ranting and was turning around to thank the major for listening when she felt *him*, and then she saw Kane, Arden, and Griffen. She wondered how long they had been there. From their faces she would say a decent amount of time.

Shit! She forced a smile on her face. "So, are we ready to go?"

She took two steps closer, looked up into Kane's face, and what she saw broke her heart. His eyes were cold as ice, his face set in stone, his body tense and rigid. He clenched his fists, and she instantly took three steps back, terrified of him for the first time in her life.

Griffen broke the silence. "Ahhhh, we thought we could take the major home so Faith could go with Kane."

She took another step back, bumping into Major Black. He grabbed her arms to steady her. She waited for the growl from Kane but heard none. She knew tears were rolling down her cheeks, and she took a deep breath.

"Look, I don't know how much you all heard, but can

we please talk about this at home?"

She felt the major touch her again, then he touched her head. She took a step forward and suddenly felt faint. She took another step toward Kane only to feel herself fall.

Chapter 10

Kane didn't know what to feel, one minute he was on cloud nine, the next he was being stopped out front by Arden and Griffen to see Faith with her back turned to the major, telling him how she didn't want to be a part of his world.

Kane knew when Faith was younger she had struggled with being psychic and being called odd, weird, and so on. But he thought she had sorted all that out and accepted that she would never be what she called normal. Maybe he should have given her more time before he mated her. He should have let her choose.

Kane looked up at Faith, and knew he could do it. He loved her enough to let her go, so she could have her normal life. He thought of the child she carried, but he could still give her a normal life as his family would help if that was what she wanted. He mentally prepared himself, resolved with what he was going to do, but it took all his strength not to growl when the major touched her. Kane tuned Faith out when he noticed the major's hand covered in blood. He knew that wasn't there when he came in.

The major touched Faith's head again, coming away

with more blood. Kane quickly looked at Faith as she took a step toward him. Her arms were covered in blood and she was white as a sheet. He rushed, using wolf speed to get to her, but didn't make it before she fell to the ground. He would never forget the sound of her body hitting the concrete. He roared in terror. They all surrounded her, and he kind of blacked out. He remembered yelling for someone to go in and get Dr. Stark. He knelt beside her, not letting anyone touch her until he knew the best doctor was coming. Jerome came out and took in the situation, asking Kane about her medical history and what had happened. It was Arden who remembered to add she was pregnant. Kane made sure Jerome knew that she was first priority over the fetus. He quickly calculated a due date as werewolf pregnancies took only six months instead of nine.

Twenty-five minutes later, he sat with his brothers in the waiting room while a five-year resident student came out to give them their fourth update. This one looked hesitant as he slowly walked over to them. Kane didn't blame the guy, they looked like a pretty intimidating bunch, twenty to twenty-five massive werewolves with more family coming in.

"Ahh, Dr. Wolfen, they're just finishing up in the operating room. Dr. Stark will be out in a moment. They had to take caution as from the scans we could tell it had just missed the brain."

He nodded as the student rushed away. Calmed a bit at knowing it was almost over, he looked to Arden first for answers. "How far away is Dad?"

Arden shrugged. "Five minutes to ten minutes tops."

Kane nodded then turned to Major Black. "What the hell happened?"

The major cleared his throat and told the event the best he could in a public place.

Once he had finished explaining what had happened Kane felt his father's hand on his back. Furious, he turned and slammed him against the wall. Plaster smashed, and everyone froze as alpha-to-alpha he got right up in his face.

In a harsh whisper, he growled, "What the hell were you thinking letting my wife, my pregnant wife, go out with only four werewolves and a fucking human? You would never have let my mother, your mate, do anything that dangerous, pregnant or not. I know you didn't know she was pregnant, but she still shouldn't have gone out. You don't let any of the women in the pack fight, and they're shifters. Why did you let my little human mate fight? Faith almost died, but thanks to me mate marking her it gave her extra strength and healing skills which saved her, but now we have to fucking cover it up." He spoke the last statement loud so all the werewolves could hear. Without even giving his father a chance to respond, he let him fall to the floor and walked away, not caring what excuse he came up with.

A minute later the nurse came and collected him, but before he left he turned so all could hear. "Keep Rane away from me. Father, I stopped myself from killing you by a thread, but that won't be there for him. If Rane had done what he was ordered to do and kept the major with him, instead of Faith having to watch his behind, this wouldn't have happened."

* * * *

Faith awoke slowly to a splitting headache and looked around the unfamiliar room. She tried to remember what had happened but the last thing she could remember was waking up in Kane's arms before he had to go to work. She tried harder, clutching her head in pain. She started to freak out, looking frantically for something, anything she could remember. She heard the toilet flush as she cried out, "Kane! Please, where are you, Kane?" She felt him then as he came running out of the bathroom.

"Princess, I'm here. I'm here, calm down."

She clung to his hand. "Please, don't leave me. What happened?"

He kissed her forehead as a nurse came rushing in. Kane barked for her to call Dr. Stark, and the nurse hurried off to do Kane's bidding.

He turned back to Faith. "I've never been so afraid in my whole life, Faith." He sat on the bed, carefully bringing her into a hug. "I love you so much."

Faith snuggled closer to Kane. "I love you too, Kane. I have never, will never, love anyone else. I'm so sorry if I scared you, but I don't remember how I got here."

Kane hugged her tighter. "You don't remember your vision or helping the women? This…" He touched her head. "…that you have now was a gift, you could say, from a demon."

She touched her head which had a bandage around it.

"Faith, you took on a demon pretty much all by yourself, and I know you helped kill a second, but princess..." He shook his head just as a knock sounded on the door.

Faith looked up to see a tall black man, about six feet one, with broad shoulders and one of the most handsome faces she had seen. If she didn't know better she would swear he had the genes of a were. Her paranormal gift came in handy helping her find and know paranormal people, and she knew this man wasn't a shifter, but she was picking up that he had some sort of paranormal gift, she just couldn't figure out what it was.

He grinned at her, showing perfect white teeth. "Hi, Faith. I'm Dr. Jerome Stark. How are you feeling? You're a very lucky woman."

Faith smiled, wincing in pain. "Nice to meet you, Dr. Stark. I'm not feeling that hot, my head is throbbing."

"That's to be expected when a woman has a claw removed from the back of her head. You're lucky it hadn't embedded in your brain. You're even luckier to have such remarkable healing abilities."

Kane shot the doctor a shut-the-fuck-up look.

"I would have liked for you to stay a day or two so I could monitor you and make sure everything heals well, but with the military clearance and having a doctor as a husband we'll get you on your way home in an hour or two."

Kane spoke up. "Jerome, she's forgotten the past twenty-four hours, but I think she did well to only forget that much."

Jerome nodded to him and looked at Faith. "What's the last thing you remember?"

She smiled. "The last thing I remember is hugging Kane this morning, groaning about losing my heater, and begging him to stay before I pushed him out of bed or he would have given in to me."

The doctor smacked Kane on the back of the head. Kane turned. "What the hell did you do that for?"

Dr. Stark glared at Kane. "Because if I had a wife like this I would have stayed in bed." He turned his focus on her. "Faith, if you ever come to your senses about this idiot give me a call. I would gladly take his place."

Faith giggled. "Thank you, Dr. Stark. I'll have to think about that."

He chuckled and came over to check her out, taking off the bandage. She breathed a sigh of relief as her hair tumbled down. He chuckled again.

"Yes, I tried to save as much of your beautiful hair as I could, but the bottom half is shaved." He gently lifted her head. "Unbelievable. You'll be going home—with a military escort, I understand—as soon as I can do the paperwork. And somehow your husband has now been cleared for indefinite leave." He shook his head then looked at Kane. "Don't worry, I will be calling." He smiled at her again and left.

Kane said nothing for a long time and just stared at her. When she couldn't take the silence anymore she sat up. "Where is everyone? I thought at least Jamie would have been here to see if I'm okay."

His face never changed from his deep-in-thought expression as he said, "They would have all been here if they were allowed, but you need your rest, so rest, Faith." He walked out the door.

Something was up. Everything felt very wrong.

* * * *

At home the feeling got worse as Kane placed her on the bed, kissed her forehead again, not her lips, and left, telling her to sleep. She lay in bed for fifteen minutes, and the sense of wrongness just got worse. She had never seen Kane like this. The whole ride home from the hospital he hadn't said a word, even when she asked if he was okay. She asked if she could help make anything better, but he was so emotionless. Sitting up, she tried to feel for him with their bond, but like when she had tried in the car, she got nothing.

She shivered and slipped out of the room. She headed for his study. Before she opened the door she heard him say, "I want her out. I don't fucking care. I'll find a way to resolve the mate claim. She's human, that should help." Faith couldn't hold back the wince at the last comment. "If she can stay the fuck away from me for over four years she can do it again. I'll set her and the baby up so she has no worries. You all can help her, just don't let her get involved anymore in paranormal shit."

Faith took a step back, placing her hand over the child she now knew grew there. She shut her eyes, concentrating. Yep, she was pregnant, he was definitely there. She was too shocked with what she had heard to be angry with Kane for not telling her. Her heart was in a million pieces.

"No, once she's recovered I'll be heading to Canberra. I'll lead the enforcers up there for a couple of years."

Faith couldn't stand to hear any more. She snuck quietly back to their room. She needed to leave. She knew she was taking the coward's, the selfish, way out by not confronting him, but she couldn't break her heart again and again for Kane Wolfen. She found her cellphone and called her friend to come pick her up.

Faith walked out the door five minutes later with a backpack full of clothes. Fifteen minutes later Remy came to pick her up. Only then did she ring Della, Kane's mother, telling her she was safe and staying with a friend, and she would come get Bengie tomorrow. She hung up before Della could ask any questions. Faith rung her parents and told them she was staying with a friend for a couple of weeks. Faith then called the mobile she'd gotten for Bengie, telling him she was fine, she loved him, and to call if he needed her, but otherwise she would see him tomorrow.

After they arrived at Remy's house, Remy left her in peace for a day, then, in true Remy style, she came storming into the room, joining Faith on the bed where she had been sulking. "What the fuck did the cradle-robbing dick do to you this time?"

Faith couldn't hold it in any longer, she broke down and told Remy everything, swearing her to secrecy. Faith knew Remy would believe her story, because Faith kept Remy's secret about being a fire element. The only thing Faith left out was what Bengie really was.

Remy looked shocked, terrified, and angry. "I knew there was a reason why I fucking stayed away from them."

"Remy, they save the world, they're good. I love them, they're my family."

Remy sighed then hugged her. "Sounds like you save the world too. How do you feel about that?"

As soon as Remy asked that question the last twenty-four hours came back to Faith. Sick to her stomach, she rushed to the bathroom and threw up. When she finished Remy helped clean her up, then Faith answered her question. "I truly don't know how I feel. I need time to get my priorities in order." She placed her hand over the baby growing inside her, which she had only just found out about thanks to her psychic powers. She looked straight into

Remy's eyes. "I need to grow up, and not just for me."

Remy nodded, and they fell asleep hugging each other.

* * * *

Kane went to the bedroom to check on Faith. He knew he'd been too cold with her, but he had to start distancing himself from her if he was going to give her the normal life she wanted. He knew it was going to kill him, especially now that she was pregnant with his child, but he wanted her to be happy. Kane took a deep breath before entering the room, which was empty. Calling her name, he checked the bathroom, then walked to the lounge and finally into the kitchen. On the fridge he saw a note.

Dear Dr. Wolfen,

I'm out. There is no need for you to move to Canberra. As you said, I'm human. I will avoid you like I have for four years. I will not do this again with you. Thanks for the lesson. You have made me stronger. I won't get burnt again. You may see your son whenever you want, within reason. Your parents can be the go-between. I don't need your help to set me up.

Good luck,

Faith York

P.S: I will look after my brother, and I will pick up his stuff when I find a place.

Kane sat on the floor against the fridge. He reread the note several times. He went over his conversation with his father again and again. By the sound of the letter, he knew she had heard part of the conversation. He sat there until the sun rose. He had a sense of déjà vu. He went through the conversation Faith had with the major. His mind was on a twenty-four hour loop. His wolf was howling, ripping at its cage to get out and find its mate, he couldn't go without her again. Kane got up, knowing he needed to find his brothers, he needed to know the full conversation with the major.

None of his brothers answered their phones. He tried going around to Arden and Griffen's but they wouldn't open the door. He pulled the big guns in then…he called his mother. "Hi, Mum. Can y—"

"What have you done to her this time, Kane? I thought I raised you better."

He winced and almost didn't ask his favor. "Mum, is Ben there?"

His mother sighed. "No, Faith has taken him out. He'll

be back tonight. I told her we'd keep him until she finds a place, but Kane, it better bloody well not come to that."

Kane put his head in his hands. "Look, Mum, I'm coming around. Can you call my brothers, please? I need to talk to them."

"You better make it right. Give me ten minutes."

* * * *

By the time Kane reached his parents' house he knew all his brothers were there bar Rane. His mother opened the door and batted him on the head whilst telling him they were all in the den. He walked in to see his brothers glaring at him.

"Look, I know you're angry," Kane said, "but I need you to tell me the whole conversation Faith had with the major."

Arden's answer was immediate. "Fuck you, Kane. I renounce you. You're an arsehole to her every time. I don't know why you got the privilege to have her." He turned his back on him.

Kane stared at Arden, shocked by his words. He mentally shook his head, trying to help himself focus on the problem at hand and not Arden, who had always been his number one supporter. He turned to Griffen. "Come on, Grif. Please. I beg you, and I never beg."

Sneering at him, Griffen replied, "What does it matter? It shouldn't, and you know it. All you have to do is look at her and her actions over the last fourteen to fifteen years she's known you. I shouldn't have to say this, but she shines. We aren't the only ones drawn to it, let's just say it was a lot of trouble to keep the wolves we sent to just check on her, they all fell in love with her and wanted her for their own. I know for a fact she turned down many offers for dates."

Kane shut his eyes, trying to get all the images out of his head.

Jamie spoke up. "I talked to her."

His eyes shot open. "Where is she, Jamie? I need to—"

Jamie lunged, punching him. "You don't need to do fuck. She won't tell me where she is. She made sure none of us were around when she picked Ben up. I will never understand why she chose you from the first day. I was the one who saved her, I love her, but every time she chooses you. Do you want to know the thing that pisses me off the most? No matter what you do to her she still loves you. This is what she said when she called… 'I'm just ringing to say not to bother coming around. Kane doesn't want me for a mate, so I'm going to give him what he wants and leave. When I get settled you can come and protect me. Don't worry, I'm safe. I love you. Please be nice to Kane, try to look after him for me...' She wouldn't let me get a word in, then she hung up and turned off her phone."

Devlin chimed in. "Tell him, Arden. Tell him what was said."

Arden looked at Devlin. "Are you crazy?"

He shook his head. "Look at him. Look at our cool, collected alpha brother Dr. Kane Wolfen."

Arden looked him over then started. "She said, and I quote, 'I came back from overseas and straightaway I'm thrown back into all this, and mated to Kane, who I love with all my heart. I would gladly go through anything just to be with him. I loved him from the first moment I laid eyes on him, but being thrown back into it all... My visions before I left were never this strong, long, or thorough. I'm really just trying to figure out my place in all this.' And you heard the rest."

Kane knew he was white. He sat on the floor and didn't even notice his brothers leave, he just sat and thought everything over. Kane couldn't believe his stupidity, he even remembered a lecture on head injuries, usually patients remembered what they wanted to, or from a certain point in their lives where they were happy. He banged his head on the lounge because he knew Faith remembered them snuggling in bed, her begging him not to go to work. He thought about how when she woke up in the hospital her first words were to yell for him. He laughed bitterly. She had even told him she loved him and would never love anyone else. The whole ride home she had asked if he was okay.

He shut down. He couldn't believe what he had done, he had lost her again.

Chapter 11

Faith sat outside with Remy, practicing controlling her visions.

"So have you decided what you're going to do?"

Faith smiled. She felt fantastic. For the last week she had been working out her options. She'd been to see a therapist, and she had spoken to Remy every night, telling her everything. It felt great to have a human friend that she could tell everything to. It was nice, it made her feel normal, and after a week of talking and thinking she knew without a doubt what she was going to do. "I'm going to fight. You're right, I could never live with myself if I turned my back. I know you don't want to hear this, but I've been checking on Kane. He's not doing so good. I need to see him, to tell him that I don't want to be normal, I want to be me. I want to help, and if he doesn't like it, he'll have to learn to suck it up, because I'm not going to run anymore."

Remy sighed. "I know you love him, but he's not good enough for you, Faith. All he seems to do is break your heart."

Faith shut her eyes to stop the tears. "I love you, Remy, but it wasn't all him, as they say it takes two to tango. I was childish. I stayed away from him for over four years, he was the main reason I went overseas. I need to let go of the past. I need to try, even if it's only for the baby."

"I bet you wish you could just see what was going to happen."

Faith laughed. "I wish it worked like that, but I very rarely see anything that has to do with me."

Remy frowned. "But I thought you saw those women, and you saw Brad was going to propose if you decided to start seeing him."

"It's hard to explain, but I'll start by saying that the future can always be changed. It's only the past that's set in stone. And Brad proposing will never come to pass now as I changed the future. The women I saved…I only saw three demons, but there ended up being easily double that. The frustrating thing is I only see what fate wants me to see. It's the other gifts that help. I just hope it will be enough to save us all." She looked up to see the worried look on Remy's face. Shit, she really shouldn't have said all that. "I'm so sorry to put all my trouble and worries on you."

Remy waved her hand and hugged Faith. "I asked. I'm glad you're going to help the fight, it sure does make me feel better. How about we do something fun before we pick up your brother this afternoon? Let's go shopping."

* * * *

Kane spent a week in hell. He couldn't stop thinking about everything that had happened. He needed to get Faith back, he couldn't live without her again. He was going to give her anything she wanted. Kane knew she wasn't perfect, but she was damn near perfect to him. He had tried his brothers, but none would talk to him. His sisters were worse. No one would tell him where Faith was, not even his parents. His mother had said Faith would tell him, just give her time, and his father said if he really wanted to find her he needed to think.

Today he was at his parents' house. He had finally used his brain, he grabbed Bengie before he started playing his video games, which didn't go down well. The kid had some moves. When Kane finally had him the first words out of his mouth were, "I thought you would have come after me sooner, but Faith said I'm not to tell you where she is." He sighed.

Kane smiled. "Do you want to go for a drive? Come with me to do something special first, and then we'll play a game called hot and cold."

Ben nodded, and Kane's smile grew bigger as they got in his car and speed away.

He drove first to Jake's Tattoo Parlor to get his

surprise.

An hour later they left the shop with him having a new tattoo. When they were in the car, he turned to Ben. "Now I'm going to take you to go visit your sister."

"She said I'm not to tell you where she is."

"Well, you're not really. In this game all you're going to do is say 'hot' or 'cold', 'really cold' if I'm really wrong and 'really hot' if we're almost there or close by."

Bengie smiled. "Ah, very clever."

* * * *

Two hours later Kane was really, really hot, but ten minutes ago he didn't need to play the game anymore, his wolf had taken over and he could feel the bond. They arrived out front of a quiet, tiny cottage with a reserve behind it and a blue little Beetle car out front. He let Ben go before him, knowing he would need him to get in.

Ben knocked on the door. He was so eager he was bouncing. A tiny woman answered. She was about five foot two with short blonde hair. She reminded him of what a pixie would look like. Her face lit up as soon as she saw Ben, and damn if Ben's face didn't just light up like a Christmas tree. Who would of thought?

"Ben, we were just coming to get you. Come in. Faith will be so happy to see you."

Ben walked through the door, smiling the whole time, though careful not to show his sharp teeth.

"Who's brought you this time? I know it wasn't Arden because Faith told me he went away yesterday for a couple of months." The pixie rolled her eyes. "Like I care what he does. I have never met him nor do I want to meet him anyti..." She stopped and stared at Kane as he finally came out of the shadows and tried to get inside. The little pixie shocked him with the words that came out of her mouth next. "Holy crap, you look like shit. What the hell happened to you?" Then she looked closer. "You're the motherfucker who..." She kicked him, then punched his stomach. "*Ouch*! That was for Faith." She shut the door in his face, and he heard her yell, "Faith, you're not going to believe it, but a fucking cradle-robbing psychopath is out front. You better call in reinforcement, because he looks like shit. I thought you said they weren't covered in hair. He looks like sasquatch."

Kane winced. God, she looked like a cute pixie but swore worse than a trucker. Kane knew he looked like shit. He hadn't slept in a week. He lifted up his arms and winced. Okay, so he should have showered before he came, properly shaved too based on the comment about him looking like sasquatch.

A minute later the door opened and his breath caught. Faith got more beautiful every time he saw her. She stood in the doorway, wearing a simple yellow sun dress, the pixie behind her. He could tell Faith didn't have on a bra, because as soon as she saw him her nipples hardened. He smiled as the pixie said, "Oh my God, Faith, what is it?"

Faith rolled her eyes. "Remy, you know who it is, don't be mean. Go show Bengie your garden, put him to work. I need to talk to Kane."

The pixie glared at him. "Don't hurt her or I'll kick your arse again."

He held back the chuckle and he nodded as she walked away.

"I was an idiot. I was so scared to lose you I pushed you away," he told Faith, "but I've loved you from the first moment I saw your chubby, dirty, little face. The princess who told me I would be her prince. You terrified me when I saw you in that Rapunzel outfit, because I knew then that I was in trouble. As you got older you got more beautiful, and not just on the outside, it shone from the inside out. It was getting harder to stay away from you, then when you came home I couldn't resist you anymore. I should have given you time, not just thrown you back into it all. But from the moment I saw you I've been scared of what you are and mean to me. Please, Faith, I love you. I can't live without you anymore. If that makes me selfish, then I'm selfish." He took her into his arms. He felt her tears against him, then she pushed at his chest and ran inside.

Following her, he found her vomiting into the toilet. "Princess, you okay?"

She made a lame attempt to bat him away. "Lock the door and get into the shower, Kane. Please, you stink."

She got up, brushed her teeth, and rinsed her mouth with mouthwash as she watched him in the shower. He got out and grabbed a towel that barely covered him, Faith watching him the whole time. Her eyes kept flicking back to his new tattoo.

"We both made mistakes, Kane. I've decided I want to help. I want to be me, Faith, the weird psychic woman. The woman who gets feelings, who sees things. I am going to be a woman who is going to help protect the world." She looked into his eyes. "Our son and future children will be proud of their mother. We are going to stop Armageddon. When we go back home there are going to be some changes, whether you like it or not. Our major concern should be finding those women the demons have."

She came to him, and he sighed, breathing in her scent, feeling whole again. "I have resigned from the hospital, so I can help out more. I'll feel better if I can watch your back. And I know Dad could use the help. I was really hard on him when you got hurt."

She looked up at him. "I love you so much, Kane. I just want you to be happy, but next time we fight—and there's no point denying it, you drive me too crazy for us to be in harmony all the time—can you not take up the caveman look? Because right now you're giving the movie hairy werewolves a run for their money."

Kane gave a mock growl, nipping her shoulder. Faith laughed and he beamed, loving the sound. He picked her up, kissing her. "I'm the happiest when I'm with you."

She reached down to pull the towel off him, and he wiggled his hips to loosen it, helping her. Kane grinned as she lifted her dress over her head. She had nothing on underneath, and he growled, capturing her mouth. "Fuck, you're gorgeous."

She smiled, muttering against his lips, "God, I missed you so much. I've been so cold without my heater."

He chuckled. "It's good to know I'm needed."

"I do love you, Kane, but I will still want to have a weekend where I can be a normal twenty-year-old, like go to a concert or have a girls' night out on the town, but I'm sure you can survive for one or two nights a month without me."

She smiled, and he kissed her, making sure to put all his love, loneliness, passion, and wanting into the kiss. She wrapped her arms around his neck, moving her fingers up to his hair, running them through. She whispered in his ear, "I love your new tat. You're lucky I love you, because you now have my name branded on you forever." She kissed his chest where her name was written.

Kane growled, moving her so she sat on the bathroom counter. She arched back onto the mirror as he sucked and nipped his way around her neck.

* * * *

Faith knew she was crying. She had missed Kane so much. Now that she had him back she knew she couldn't be without him again. Her heart, mind, and body craved him. All he had to do was touch her and a fire started in her veins. Her head fell back on the bathroom mirror as he sucked and nipped at her neck. She loved his mouth.

He kissed his way down her body. Pausing at her stomach, he kissed it, whispering how much he loved her and their child. He paused again between her legs. He had a huge grin on his face as he said, "Let's see if my caveman look is a hindrance or a help."

His face went straight to her clit, and he sucked it in,

swirling his tongue before he nipped. Crying out his name, Faith wrapped her legs around his shoulders, pushing his face further into her pussy. He growled his pleasure, and the vibration made her shiver in ecstasy. "Oh God, do that again."

He growled again. This time he shook his face, lapping at her pussy.

"Kane, I can't take any more. I've missed you so much. I was ready as soon as the water hit your body in the shower. Please, Kane, I need… I need."

He moved quick as lightning up her body and plunged into her aching pussy. She moaned, loving the feel of his big, fat dick ramming into her. He latched onto one of her nipples, sucking and swirling his tongue over her erect nipple. He alternated to the other, back and forth in exquisite torture. As he moved his thrusts to match the pass of his sucking she yelled out her orgasm as his fingers played with her clit. He growled, biting her nipple, and stopped to flip her over so her hands were on the bathroom vanity. He gripped her bottom to hold her up. He smacked her arse and grabbed her cheeks, giving them a good squeeze. As Kane reentered her in one quick thrust, one hand moved up to cup her breast and the other played with her nub.

Faith groaned as she looked into the mirror to see a sight that was the hottest thing she had ever seen. Kane's eyes glowed bright blue, his face had a feral pleasure look with his jaw set, his muscles flexing and straining. His pace picked up faster and harder until she was white knuckled gripping the vanity.

Kane growled. "Mine, you're mine, Faith. Always mine."

He leaned down, sucking on her neck. His eyes captured hers in the mirror, and she slammed back against him and screamed her pleasure. She could feel his dick growing impossibly bigger. He howled, clamping down on her shoulder, his hips thrusting into her as he came. Her orgasm still raking her body, she muttered, "Mmm, make-up sex rocks."

He chuckled against her shoulder. His face held a satisfied smile. He picked her up, still locked inside her. "Where's the bedroom, princess?"

She groaned as she pointed in the direction. Each step he took was pulling on the barb that locked him to her, making her pussy muscles tighten. He opened the bathroom door and she squealed, "Remy and Bengie..."

Kane chuckled. "I heard them leave out the front door as you were moaning my name twenty minutes ago."

She sighed as he laid them on the bed. Faith snuggled her back into his chest. "I love you, Kane. I missed our bed, and I can't wait to get home. I was going to come see you today. I love you so much, and I love our baby. He's going to be so handsome, just like his father. I've been practicing how to call and control my visions, and I've been doing really well. We have a lot to prepare for, but with help I know we will win."

Kane kissed her shoulder over the mate mark. "I have every confidence in you, princess, and us."

Epilogue

Kane's 35th Birthday

There was a good turnout. Twenty alphas from around the world either stood or sat in the den. Rane also counted ten military representatives. All were waiting for Faith and Kane to come in. It would seem the demons were becoming a lot more aggressive, making themselves known not just in Australia. They had all underestimated them. It was late November, and Faith had been back now for a month and a half. Kane had put a whole heap of blame for Faith's potentially fatal injury on Rane and their father. The argument was his dad should have somehow pulled more werewolves out of his arse and Rane should have watched Faith's back, not left her with Major Samuel Black.

The tension in the family was high, and Kane was driving everyone nuts. You would think a doctor wouldn't be so overprotective about his wife being pregnant. Speaking of the devil, Faith walked in, looking radiant in a black dress with red stilettos and matching purse with a ruby pendant and earrings. Faith turned, smiled at Rane, and winked, kissing his cheek, which made Kane growl. Everyone except Kane and Faith took a seat. Faith stared at them all then came straight to the point.

"I have seen Armageddon."

It was the wrong thing to say. Everyone talked at once. Kane's growl to "listen up" shut everyone up, especially when Faith added her whistle.

"As I was saying, I have seen Armageddon. Well, what I saw looked like it, but, and this is a big but, it can be changed from the vision I had." She looked at the military people. "The military had no idea how to work with the werewolves or how to fight the demons. What they were doing was actually giving the demons more power. The foot soldiers didn't know how to deal with them either, so they were dying, becoming slaves, food, or something equally unpleasant. Some were fighting, just not the right way. So I say for starters we need to teach our military. We need to work together, but I think the biggest help will be all the supernaturals working together. A major thing, which should be our number one focus, is finding the tunnels and cells of the supernatural people the demons are holding." She looked at the wolves. "They have lots of mates."

That got all the werewolves worried and angry as werewolves' true mates were sacred, precious, and rare. Only half the pack, if they are lucky, found them.

Faith smiled, seeming pleased with their reaction. "I

have seen that in the next couple of years, fate's going to step in and up the ante in your favor." Faith grinned as everyone started talking again, but she ignored them. Reaching up to pull Kane down, she kissed him and left.

Rane stared at the door where his sister-in-law had just left. Kane called for quiet, then turned to Rane and asked how the training of his six new military recruits was going. Rane nodded to Kane and took over, telling everyone about the six men who had been sent to learn how to help battle the demons.

Erin's Protector

Erin and her family are special, and because of their "gifts" they move often so people don't notice how strange things happen when they're around.

Erin's new job with a catering company takes her into a world she didn't know existed. She learns her family isn't so special after all when she's "claimed" by a werewolf. Jarrod explains that he's one of many shifters who help save the world, and she's his mate.

Unsure of her new situation, and if she has the strength to deal with it, Erin gives herself a week to see if she can fit in with this new life. Can Jarrod convince her that she's the one for him and she doesn't ever again need to move or worry about her family's gifts being discovered?

Content Warning: contains a sexy werewolf, graphic sex, strong language, and violence

Chapter 1

As they pulled in back of the big house, Erin glanced at her younger sister Amie. "Mum and Granddad believe that we can stay in this city for a while, as it's so big. They think people won't notice us if I keep my gloves on and you don't go healing anyone."

Amie got out of the car and Erin followed. "Erin, don't get your hopes up. I can't not help people. That little girl I saved was six. She had a year at best. I cured her." Amie fixed her ponytail and glared at her sister. "I feel bad that there are people out there we could be helping, and all Mother and Grandfather want us to do is hide our powers." Amie stomped her foot. "Do you know how many people these days are trying for children? You could help them, Erin."

They let the conversation drop momentarily as they walked up to their boss. He told them where they could put their bags and finish getting ready before they reported to the kitchen. They needed to get the table food prepared as the guests were arriving.

Erin put down her bag, trying not to think about the argument she'd had with her sister many times before, but something sounded different in Amie's voice. "Amie, we've discussed this before—if we were found out we would become experiments and used for things we can't even imagine."

Amie's eyes narrowed. "I don't care what you say, I'm not ever moving again. I'm going to stop running and hiding and start helping people. You can either stay with Mum and Granddad, or join me." She sighed. "I'm twenty-five, and I still live with my family. Look, I was going to tell everyone at the same time, but…I'm moving out. I got approval on a flat, and I move in on Monday." Without another word, she turned and walked out of the room.

Chucking her bag next to Amie's, Erin rushed after her, tying on her apron as she went. Right now she couldn't focus on what Amie had said—she had other things to deal with, and to make matters worse she'd forgotten to bring her gloves. She walked slowly around the party, holding the plate of food with both hands so she didn't touch anyone.

Erin had a feeling she was being watched. Thinking it was her sister trying to get her attention, she searched the crowd. She paused and froze on the spot as she stared at eyes that held her in their grip. Light brown eyes filled with lust, and something else, something she couldn't explain—it was like looking into an old, weary soul, and it slowly becoming bright again.

Erin tore her gaze away and looked down at the person those eyes belonged to. He was tall, well over six feet, and all muscle. His jet black hair was short except for the fringe that sat over his eyes. She gulped and took a step back as he gave her a dazzling smile and walked toward her. Holy crap! He was gorgeous and he was coming her way.

Distracted, Erin bumped into a chair behind her and dropped the plate she held. Averting her gaze, she looked at the woman sitting in the seat she'd crashed into. "I'm so sorry, ma'am." She reached down to help the woman get the food off her.

"Don't. Don't touch Edina, she needs another child like she needs her tail cut off."

Startled by the sharp voice telling her not to touch the woman, Erin turned to see a small, pregnant woman with brown eyes and dark hair.

"You can touch me. I don't think you could get me any more pregnant." The woman smiled and grabbed her arm. "You're here with the catering company? I bet you don't know what they've brought you into?"

Erin frowned. "I'm sorry, ma'am, but I don't know what you're talking about."

"Faith. My name is Faith, not ma'am, that makes me

sound old. I can see from your name tag you're Erin." She held out her hand and Erin looked down at it.

* * * *

Jarrod really didn't want to go to the party. He knew he had to because it was the next alpha in line's birthday party, but he was tired, and sick of celebrating birthdays. His own was coming up soon, he'd be ninety-five, and he was feeling every year. His heart and soul grew heavier with every kill he made. He hadn't been lucky enough to find his mate. He had a year, or maybe two, before they took him off enforcers for good. He was a captain, a leader, although lately he didn't feel like leading.

Taking a deep breath, he walked through the front door and out the back to the party. Everyone was there laughing and being merry. Faith had hired caterers, insisting that all the other women just relax and enjoy the party.

Searching through the crowd, he intended to find Faith and Kane so he could wish him a happy birthday and get the hell out of there. Not finding them, he groaned and moved to a corner to watch and wait for the birthday boy. Kane was never far behind Faith and if he couldn't find one he knew he wouldn't find the other.

As Jarrod looked over the crowd, he could see members from other packs had come to pay their respects, and he suspected, get the chance to talk to Faith and see if she could help them.

Jarrod nodded to his friends Rory and Angus as they walked over to join him. He knew were probably feeling the same as him as they were in the same situation—close to a hundred and no mate to save their weary soul.

Angus patted him on the back and grumbled, "I feel your pain. I don't want to be here either. I wonder if the young pup knows how lucky he is to have a mate." Angus shook his head. "Thirty-five and mated. Lucky bastard."

Rory, always the positive one, smiled. "We still have some time. Faith said that fate was turning to help us and many of us will find our mates."

Jarrod didn't want to bring down the mood by telling them he wouldn't get a mate as he was too old to go searching for one. So, he avoided answering by doing another sweep of the party. His gaze landed a girl who held a plate full of food with both her hands. She was average height, around five-six, with shiny golden hair that was bunched on top of her head in a messy ponytail. Her body was all curves—a full figured woman. She turned and his wolf sat up and howled. Bright green eyes stared at him. He looked her over again to see milky white skin and red rose lips parted in an "O" shape.

He was in motion before he even knew what was going on. Her eyes got wider and she gasped, dropping her plate on Edina. The girl went to help Edina clean the food off herself when Faith came out of nowhere, putting a stop to his woman helping Edina. He paused at that thought and breathed in the air around him, growling as honey and strawberry wafted to him. Jarrod's wolf panted, *Take her. Mate her. Mate. Mate. We have to have her.*

Stalking the woman, he heard Faith say, "I think it's best if we leave. You forgot your gloves and we can't have you touching guests."

Jarrod snarled as he came upon Faith and his mate. Faith had never been so rude. Clenching his fists and gritting his teeth, he took a deep breath of the strawberry and honey scent and told his wolf to calm down, to settle. They would have their mate now.

"No. She's not leaving, Faith." He glanced at the girl. Her nametag read *Erin*. He shot what he hoped was a smile at Erin. "She is mine. Erin's not leaving." He couldn't help the snarl in his voice and knew it would get him in trouble. His instincts told him he should step away from Faith and not tower over her, but his wolf was out of control and urging him into action.

A werewolf arm come around him, and a scream left

Erin as Kane growled, "Apologize to my mate now. No one speaks to Faith like that."

Jarrod fought his alpha's hold as Erin's screaming got louder and she fought Faith's hold. Faith struggled until Jamie came and took Erin from her.

Jarrod knew he wasn't being rational, but as soon as Jamie touched Erin his strength seemed to triple—he didn't like another male touching his mate.

Faith came up to him and let out a long sigh as a couple of werewolves held him back. "You were further gone than I thought. You still have five years until you're a hundred, but we should have seen the signs. Why didn't you say you were getting weary?"

He could barely focus on what Faith was saying; his mind and wolf were focused on the woman cowering in terror in Jamie's arms.

Faith shook her head. "I don't know why I'm talking to you. You're not going to hear a word I say until you've mated that girl. Look, I wasn't kicking her out of town. Just out of the party. Your mate is quite special, and God forbid the demons get a hold of her. She's a fertility deity. The deity part is weak, but the fertility is very strong. Anyone she's touched tonight will be warned to stay away from their mates, and any single woman will be told to have no liaisons tonight unless they want a baby." Faith stroked her own tiny stomach and grinned. "You need to calm down. You're scaring your mate." She glanced behind him. "Kane, turn back to human and let him go. Jamie, let go of Erin and move as far away from her as you can."

As soon as Jarrod was free, he went straight to his mate, who sat shaking on the ground. He picked her up and cradled her in his arms.

She shrieked and bashed at his chest. "Let me go. I promise I won't tell anyone about you. Please don't hurt me. I'll wear my gloves. Just let me go. Please, I won't say a word."

Stroking her hair with one hand, he murmured soothing words to her. "Sweetheart, I'm sorry I scared you. You're safe. No one will ever hurt you. You're precious to me. My mate. Everything's fine now, Erin. I'll protect you."

He walked out of his alpha's party, not looking back at anyone, and went straight to his house. Opening his front door, he walked directly to his room, carefully placing his mate in the middle of his bed before he stepped back and let himself take her in.

* * * *

Oh God, she'd been kidnapped by a gorgeous stranger. A possible werewolf, if she hadn't been having some weird hallucination, or a crazy episode. No human would be able to fight against the massive creatures he had to get to her and not get hurt. Erin didn't know what to think about what she had just seen, but she was terrified and intrigued at the same time. Her mind was going over everything that she thought was normal.

She'd thought that she and her family were the only supernatural people around. They'd moved from town to town, city to city, to avoid people noticing the unusual things that happened when they were around. Erin had the worst of it. If she touched someone without gloves on, and they had sex within the next couple of days, they became pregnant. The more time she touched that person, the higher the certainty. Anyone she touched for a long time usually ended up with twins or triplets. So she wore gloves all the time.

Her mother and sister Amie had the power to heal people. Their granddad was a walking lie detector. She had always thought her family was alone.

Erin eyed the werewolf before her. He had short, dark black hair, a nice tan to his olive skin, a sharp nose, and full lips. But it was his eyes that captured her, they were like warm light chocolate, making her melt inside. Shaking her head to stop herself from falling under his spell, she looked around at the white walls and sparsely decorated room. "Where am I?"

"You're at my house in my...*our* room."

She sat herself back against the wall. "I guessed that I was at your house. I mean what is this town? Are you all werewolves? Did I just see what I think I did? Because I've never been so terrified in my life. I just saw werewolves. Wow, I thought my family was unusual."

"Yes, you did see werewolves. You're looking at one right now." He moved closer to the bed. She plastered herself against the wall and he halted. "Erin, I would never hurt you. I'd gladly give up my life for you."

"You didn't answer my question."

He raked his fingers through his hair. "This is a werewolf town. Well, we were, but lately a lot of other supernaturals have decided to live here in order to stay safe, but they're on the other side of town. There's also a military base just before you hit town which has some humans."

Erin couldn't believe what she was hearing. "How many werewolves and other supernaturals are there?"

He sat on the end of the bed. "There are thousands of werewolves and other shifters, and we don't know the number of supernatural people. But if you talk to Faith she'll tell you that everyone has some supernatural sense."

Erin's whole world was changing. She pulled her legs up and hugged them to her stomach. She studied the werewolf who stared at her like he could eat her up. His brown eyes were alight with lust and passion. His hands were fisted in the bedsheets and she could hear his heavy breathing.

"Why am I at your house? Why did you take me? I don't know you. I don't even know your name."

He inched closer to her and brushed some hair that had fallen out of her ponytail and into her eyes. "My name's Jarrod, and you are my mate. My wolf and I knew as soon as we laid eyes on you that you are ours. And as we got closer, your honey and strawberry scent surrounded me and helped confirm what you are to me." His lips brushed over hers, and he moved her away from the wall and further down the bed. "You, gorgeous, will get to know me well. I have waited years for you. I have dreamed of finding you. I've fantasized about everything I would do to you."

Erin lay on the bed and tried to calm her heart as it beat faster and her breaths come out in pants. Jarrod was so close to her now that his fresh, woodsy smell drugged her senses, and her skin prickled as his body came to rest over hers.

He tilted her chin up to meet his eyes. "You, Erin, are mine. Tonight I'm going to show you why we were made for each other. Why you are the other half of my soul."

Jarrod slid off the bed and stood up, pulling his shirt off and throwing it to the ground. Her eyes widened at his muscular chest, and she squeezed her eyes shut for a moment as heat stole her body. Opening her eyes, she groaned as he wiggled his pants down and they pooled at his feet. Wow, he went commando, and oh my, he was hard everywhere. She scrambled back as she looked down at his long, thick erection.

Jarrod winked when she gasped at the size of him, and he got back onto the bed and pulled her into his arms. He captured her mouth and his tongue sought entry as his hands ripped her white uniform shirt and black pants off. Her body came alive and she grabbed at him, needing what he had to offer.

In the back of her mind Erin knew something wasn't right. She'd never reacted to anyone like this. She wasn't the type of girl who had sex with a man she'd only just met. But as Jarrod's mouth left hers and he trailed kisses and little nips down her neck, she told herself that just this once it wouldn't hurt. She didn't even want to think about the fact that he was a werewolf and he thought she was his mate. *Live in the crazy moment.*

Jarrod's hands brushed over her nipples before he

leaned down and took one into his mouth. His hands snaked down her stomach, leaving tingling heat in their wake, coming to rest at the juncture between her thighs. When she arched up, his fingers slid further down and he rubbed her clit.

Jarrod growled against her skin, and she closed her eyes as delicious shivers ran through her body. "You taste so good. I'm going to eat you all up."

Erin's eyes snapped open, and she stared into his greedy, hunger filled eyes as he looked up at her from between her legs.

Jarrod licked her until she begged for release and still he didn't stop. A finger eased into her and pumped in and out. Erin gripped his hair and pushed down on his face, needing to come. He added an extra finger and gave a gentle nip to her clit, and she yelled as bliss washed over her.

He crawled up her body with a huge grin on his face. "You're gorgeous. This time when you come I want to see the ecstasy I give you."

Jarrod's cock slowly, achingly, eased into her, and she wrapped her legs around him and slipped her arms around him. He was bigger than she'd had before, and she took deep breaths as she felt herself stretching. Jarrod nibbled at her neck, and his hands glided up and down her body, leaving trails of burning need. He nipped at her ear, which sent shivering thrills coursing through her.

When he was fully seated inside her, he paused, and his gaze captured hers before he eased out and then slammed back in. She gasped and gripped him tight as he hit just the right spot. Jarrod kept pumping into her, his eyes never leaving hers.

"You're mine, Erin. I will make love to you until the end of our time. Mine."

Jarrod's pace picked up, and his hands grabbed her arse and pushed her up to meet each of his thrusts. She gripped him tighter, her nails digging into his skin.

A loud snarl escaped him and he growled before diving for her neck. He licked it once, twice, and then bit down hard as he pistoned into her.

Erin let out a scream as the biggest orgasm she'd ever had in her life exploded through her. Delicious, elation, euphoria settled over her. Her hands moved down to rest on his butt as he pushed in one last time and let go of her neck to howl his release.

Erin moaned as blissed paradise settled over her as the base of his dick thicken so much it locked her to him. Utterly spent, she sagged back into the bed. "Holy crap, once you go werewolf there's no way you'll go back."

Jarrod chuckled as he hugged her to him, moving them to snuggle on their side. She could feel his cock pulsing inside her. She tried to sit up, but he held her to him tight.

"Sweetheart, you're my mate. I mated you, which means any time we make love I'll lock inside you for a good twenty minutes."

She sighed, content. "At least you won't get out of snuggling afterward."

Jarrod let out a deep belly laugh. He leaned down and kissed the place where he'd bitten her. "I'm a lucky man. I'm glad you see the positive."

She was wrung out with everything that had happened, and all she could do was nod. As she drifted off to sleep, she told herself she'd ask more questions when she woke.

Chapter 2

Jarrod looked down at his mate as she slept in his arms. He knew he was lucky to have found her, and just in time too—his wolf was becoming feral and his soul was getting heavy. His wolf was calm now for the first time in years and he felt light, like a weight had been lifted off his shoulders.

Jarrod knew he'd moved fast for a human. He hoped she didn't want to leave him, because he didn't know if he could handle that, he'd hadn't known until he saw her last night how close he was to becoming feral. Jarrod had to convince her stay, even if he had to fight dirty.

Anytime she'd made a move to leave, he'd distracted her, using any means possible. He wasn't giving her up. He refused to go back to the bleak state he was in before meeting her. It hadn't even been twenty-four hours and he already felt better than he had in years.

Erin groaned and snuggled into him more. Jarrod stroked her hair and savored the feeling of her in his arms. She stretched before slowly sitting up. For a moment she seemed dazed then she let out a squeak and pulled the covers up over her body.

"Oh God, it wasn't some crazy dream. You're real. I

need to call my family and tell them I'm okay. I need to go." Erin jumped out of bed with the sheet wrapped around her.

Jarrod didn't care about his nudity as he got up and pulled Erin back to bed. "Call your family later. I have things I have to do to you first."

She stared up at him. "Um, what do you have to do?" She looked worried.

Taking the bedsheet from her body, he growled against her skin and she shivered. "This."

Erin's shriek turned into a moan as he moved his hands down her body and eased two fingers into her, sliding them in and out. His mouth covered hers, and their tongues met, tangling together.

Jarrod flipped them so Erin was on top. He eased his mouth from hers and rasped out, "Ride me."

She grinned and moved down until she hovered over his erection, then slowly slid down onto him. Erin's head fell back as she seated herself fully. She looked like a fallen angel—her hair was wild and messy, falling in golden waves around her, her small pink lips were parted, and her eyes were hooded in a blissed filled state.

Jarrod knew he must have a stupid grin on his face. He was in heaven, watching her tits bounce as she lifted up and came down. Reaching up, he cupped them. He rubbed his thumbs over her nipples and she let out a whimper. Moving a hand down her stomach to rest on her hip, he helped her pick her pace up. She started slamming down on him and grounding into him.

Jarrod let go of her breast and trailed the fingers of his other hand down her stomach and rubbed her clit. Erin groaned and murmured for him not to stop. He lifted his hips up to meet her as she sank down onto his dick, and he delved deeper into her core. As he pressed down harder on her nub, she arched into his touch. He watched as she came apart. Throwing her back, she screamed her release. Her pussy muscles quivered around him, and he pushed up one last time, grunting as he felt the base of his cock expand and he came undone.

Erin came down on top of him, hugging him to her. He could hear her panting for breath. "You're going to have to explain things. One of the best things about you locking in me is that you can't get away."

He chuckled and kissed her forehead. "I'm glad you think that's the best part."

* * * *

Erin eased herself up, crossing her arms over his chest, and looked at Jarrod. "I have a lot of questions. For instance, how have you stayed secret with all the new technology? Does the government know? Are you classed as human? What does it mean to be a shifter? Can I see you change into a full wolf? Do you change into a full wolf? Will I turn into one now that you've bitten me?"

Jarrod smiled at her. "Are those all of the questions?"

She shrugged, and then her body shivered as she could still feel the effects of her pussy pulsing. "For now."

His arms came around her and his hands rested on her arse cheeks. "The government knows about us. A lot of us are in the government all over the world. What's helped us with the technology part is having an 'in' with all government agencies. We think of ourselves as human sometimes, but most of the time we just call ourselves shifters or paranormal."

Jarrod's hands rubbed over her body and she let her fingers draw circles on his chest.

"You won't turn into a werewolf. You have to be born one. But my bit mark tells everyone you're my mate. It will help you to heal quicker, run faster, and make you stronger. It also extends your life. So you'll live the same length of time I do. Which is at least another hundred and fifty years hopefully."

She gasped and felt her eyes widen. "Oh my God. How

old are you now?"

His eyes didn't meet hers and he cleared his throat several times. "I'm ninety-five, which isn't that old in werewolf years."

"You're ancient."

He growled and swatted one of her arse cheeks. "I'm young enough to keep up with you. To protect you. To make love to you until you beg me to stop."

"Oh, really?"

Jarrod gave her a wicked grin and winked at her as he slowly moved. She groaned and he sat up, cupping her face in his hands. "Erin, you're extremely important to me. We werewolves and other shifters are the world's protectors. There is a lot you don't know." He let out a breath and she could hear how heavy it was. "There are creatures called demons and they've been trying to take over the world for many years, but we shifters were made to kill them and save earth. If we find a mate, shifters live for about two hundred and fifty years. One hundred if we don't find our mate or go feral. It's said our soul slowly dies if we don't have a mate to share our burden with."

Erin couldn't believe what she was hearing. "Are you saying I'm this mate person to share your burden and grow old with?"

He nodded and she tried to push herself off. She needed to think. Erin didn't know if she could do what he was asking. "Let me go. That's a lot to ask when I just met you."

Jarrod held her tight. "Give us a week. If I can't convince you by next Monday lunch time, I'll let you go." He brushed his lips over hers. "Let me show you how grateful I'll be if you give me a chance."

He nipped at her throat and she moaned out, "A week."

She felt him smile against her skin as he kissed his way down her body.

* * * *

It was late afternoon and Jarrod had cooked dinner, and they were relaxing in bed after another round of sex when he heard an angry werewolf.

"Fuck." He smelt Angus before he banged on his front door and yelled.

"I'm coming in, Jarrod. Make sure you cover your mate, because I'm coming to speak to her."

He snarled and hopped out of bed. Going to his drawer, he grabbed a shirt. He came back to the bed and put it on Erin.

"Why does he want to talk to me? He won't hurt me, will he? He sounds angry."

Jarrod wondered what was wrong with his friend. Thinking it best Erin stay put until he knew the situation, he kissed her and said, "I'll be right back. Stay here. I'm going to go check it out first. I won't let anything happen to you."

He walked into his lounge room to see Angus standing at his window overlooking the water.

"Where's your mate? I need to talk to her now."

He looked into his friend's eyes to see them glowing. Shit. Angus was on the edge of going feral. Jarrod didn't want him anywhere near his mate. "She's sleeping. Why do you need to talk to her?"

Angus started to grow and change. "She has to tell me where the girl she came with lives."

He groaned as Erin come out in only his shirt. "What do you want with my sister?"

Angus's eyes narrowed, and he stalked toward Erin.

Jarrod stepped in front of her to stop him. "Don't come any closer. I don't like the look you're giving my mate. I don't want to hurt you, friend."

Angus paused and eyed him before letting out a grunt. "I would never hurt my mate's sister."

Erin gasped behind him and peeked around him. "Jarrod told me what mates are. My sister is special to you? Important to you?"

Angus nodded. "I need her to live."

Erin came from around him. "Okay, I'll take you to her, but you have to promise you'll never hurt her."

"I would never hurt her. She is my angel. My savior."

Erin reached for Angus's hand and smiled at him. "Her name is Amie. Let me shower and get dressed, and I'll take you to her."

Angus's body shrunk back to human size and he whispered, "Thank you. She ran off before I could claim her."

Chapter 3

Erin's house was half an hour drive away. The sun was just sinking as they got into Jarrod's car and she instructed him on where to go. The three of them were quiet during the ride. Erin let her hand rest on his thigh and he had his arm around her. She loved that he touched her at every opportunity.

As they pulled up in front of her family's small one-story house Erin turned to Angus. "Amie's not like me. She's not afraid to say what she feels and can be stubborn with her convictions. You said she ran from you and that's not like her. Just a warning, if she doesn't want you she'll tell you."

Angus nodded. "She ran before I could talk to her. You were busy fighting with Faith. She saw that something was going on and ran off. I chased her but she drove away before I could catch her."

As they got out of the car Erin's mother and grandfather came out to meet her. Angus didn't even let her introduce him before he pushed past them and into the house.

Her granddad huffed. "Why did you bring them here,

Erin? Amie told us what happened."

She hugged her mum and ignored her grandfather. "Mum, there are more people like us. We don't have to hide." She eased out of her mother's embrace and reached for Jarrod. "This is Jarrod. I'm his mate. He's a werewolf. There are a lot of shifters, and they save the world from demons."

Her grandfather paled and gripped her mother's arm. "There are creatures that fight those things?" he rasped.

"Yes, I've been fighting and killing them for about eighty years. How have you seen one and survived or not been captured?" Jarrod asked.

Shocked, Erin stared at her family. Her mother looked white as a sheet. "You have an aunt, or you had one. She was taken by a demon when I was pregnant with Amie. I escaped, barely, and went straight to my dad. He's stayed with us ever since, and he even distracted them once when we left a city."

Erin didn't know how she felt. Her brain was in information overload. She was still trying to process everything Jarrod had told her, and now more secrets from her mum. "I thought we always left because our powers had been discovered?"

Her mother sighed and held her hand. "Let's go inside.

I think you need to be told the truth."

Keeping a hold on Jarrod's hand, she followed her mother and granddad into the house. Once they entered they could hear arguing coming from Amie's room. Jarrod chuckled behind her.

* * * *

It was late by the time they had finished talking. Amie had come out of her room about half an hour after they started talking. She didn't look happy and as she joined in the conversation she only seemed to get worse.

A knock sounded on their front door and Steven, Erin's grandfather, went to answer it. They heard a choked cry of "Run."

Angus and Jarrod came to attention straight away and ran toward the door. "Stay here," Jarrod yelled at them.

Erin, her sister, and mother, stayed for a moment before curiosity got the better of them. Following the men outside, Erin screamed at the sight before her. Ugly looking pig-bat like creatures flew around Angus and Jarrod. They had big machetes that they were using to kill the creatures. A gray man lay on the ground. There was no blood around his corpse but his head was detached from his body.

She saw her granddad fighting with another gray man, and without thinking, she went to help. Her sister and mother ran behind her. Kicking and punching, using anything they could, together they got her grandfather free and that was when she saw them—massive demons, sixteen or seventeen feet tall. They were bright red with sharp, black thorns covering their bodies. The group of three came straight for her and her family. She tried to escape, but wasn't quick enough. The biggest demon grabbed her with his meaty hand around her neck.

The demons surrounded her family, the big one holding her tight in his grip. Jarrod and Angus ran at the one who held her in its grasp. Their huge werewolf forms were only half the size of the demons. The demon who held her dug his claws into her neck, and she felt blood trickle down her throat.

The three demons laughed, and it sounded like nails raking on a chalkboard. The one holding her spoke. "Quit while you still live, wolves. There is only two of you and three of us."

Minions attacked her family, and Erin fought to free herself from the demon's hold. Amie screamed, and Angus howled and threw himself at the demon holding Erin, going straight for the creature's heart. He pulled it out and the demon seemed shocked. He dropped her, and Jarrod helped her up and pushed her behind him as the other two demons come for them.

Straightening her shoulders and standing tall, she got ready to fight. If she was going to die, she would die fighting. Erin wasn't going to be captured. She shot a quick glance at Amie to see she'd come to the same conclusion.

Jarrod shoved a knife into her hand and yelled, "Their head has to come off, and their heart has to come out. Watch for their tail."

With that, he ran at one demon while Angus climbed on the back of the one he'd taken the heart out of. The third demon was trying to pull Angus off. She could hear sirens in the distance and gave a quick glance at Jarrod before she ran to help Angus, distracting the demon who was trying to pull him off the biggest one's back. A two pointed arrow tail slithered toward her and she slashed at it. The sirens were getting closer, and she prayed help was on the way.

Erin screamed as a tail wrapped around her waist, sticking into her stomach. Squealing in pain, she cut the tail off and ran at the demon who had Angus by the waist. While the demon was distracted she started climbing up his back only to scream again as bullets flew past her and into the demon, who laughed and started to grow.

She looked around her street to see people coming to her family's aid with knives, rakes, wooden fence palings, and any weapons they could find. Knowing her family had help, she ignored the pain from the thorns covering the demon's body and continued to climb.

* * * *

The stupid fucking humans kept shooting the demons, and the demons grew, their strength and height increasing from the lead and steel being pumped into their bodies, making it harder for him and Angus to fight them. Jarrod was too scared to look at Erin, because he knew that would distract him.

He sighed in relief when the shooting stopped, and Tray, Sebastian, Jamie, Devlin, and Blake charged in to help.

Jamie grinned up at him. "I heard you needed some help, old man. Is the demon too much for one as old as you?"

Jarrod snarled at Jamie, and the little shit grinned and winked before running around to the back of the demon and climbing up it.

Tray came up next to him. As Jarrod dodged a demon's clawed hand, Tray looked him over and growled, "You look like shit. Go help your mate and her family. I've got this. I have some tension to let out. Although, I'd help her first as her family is doing quite good with the neighbors' help, and

Angus's mate has a vicious streak." Tray took his place cutting chunks of the demon.

Glancing around, Jarrod howled as he found his mate on a demon's back with her hands wrapped around its neck. Rushing to get there before she cut the head off and a big amount of demon acid blood got on her, he watched in growing horror as Devlin passed bigger blades up to her and told her to slice the demon's head off by hugging his neck and pulling the knives to her.

Erin yelled, "Fuck." And sliced the demon's head off. Blood squirted out, and she screamed in pain.

As Erin screamed, Jarrod climbed up the demon's back and yanked her off. Blake caught her and ran off with her. Jarrod used his long knives to finish the job Erin had started. He watched as the demon's head dropped to the ground. He heard the creature's heart shatter, and then its body fell to the floor as he jumped down.

Searching the now growing crowd, he looked for Erin. He could see Sebastian helping her family, and Angus had Amie in his arms. His wolf was getting worried, and then he spotted Kane, Blake, and Erin. She lay on an ambulance bed. He rushed over, pushing people out of the way. Erin was covered in blood and her breathing was labored. She reached for his hand, and he could see even though she'd mated him she wasn't healing quick enough.

Kane's fingers seemed to be flying as he cleaned her up and did his best. Kane looked up at him, and he could see the pitying look in his eyes.

"No! She has to be okay, I mated her. She's healing." Jarrod felt like his heart was breaking as Erin tried to smile at him. She couldn't leave him. She couldn't leave her family. He remembered Faith telling him Erin's family were healers. "Get her mother and sister. They're healers," he shouted.

"Jarrod, I don't know if they'll be able to do much," Kane whispered. "She's in bad shape, and her sister and mother aren't in much better condition. Her mother isn't mated to one of us."

Jarrod snarled and hugged Erin holding her tightly against him. "They'll try. They have to try."

Kane nodded, and a mother's cry sounded behind him. "My baby." Tanya pushed him out of the way and held Erin to her. Tanya started to glow and gradually the light dimmed.

"Pull her off," Kane roared. "She's killing herself."

It sank in that her mother was giving her child her life. Yanking the woman by the waist, Jarrod pulled her off. Her skin was gray and she was barely breathing. Kane put a breathing ventilator over her mouth.

Behind him, Angus struggled to hold Amie, who was fighting him, trying to escape his grasp. Erin shot up on a gasp only to choke on a sob as she looked down at her mother in Jarrod's arms.

Kane wouldn't stop swearing. Jarrod looked around to see Jamie holding back a tearful Steven. Angus held Amie tight with a determined look on his face.

Kane gave a long, drawn-out sigh, closed his eyes, and said, "Angus, let her come to her mother. You can pull her back as soon she's helped enough to keep her mother alive. Then we can slowly make her better."

"Would you let Faith do this if she had this healing gift?" Angus asked, and Jarrod cringed at the question.

"No, I wouldn't, but you all know Faith. She'd find a way to do it, and if I didn't let her she'd never forgive me. Angus, she's their mother, and they love her. You need to let Amie help."

Angus looked down at Amie before slowly walking toward them. He let go of Amie's waist and held her hand. Amie shimmered and stroked her mother's cheek. Tanya started breathing without the mouthpiece Kane had put on her. As soon as Tanya was breathing shallowly, Angus snatched Amie back and held her in his arms.

They could all see his wolf close to the surface. "I'm taking Amie home now." And with that he turned and walked to one of the SUVs that backup had arrived in.

Steven yelled, "Isn't anyone going to stop him?"

Kane glared at Erin's granddad. "Let Steven go, Jamie."

Jamie released him. Steven looked at Tanya then at the direction Amie and Angus had gone.

"Go after him. I dare you," muttered Jamie.

Steven groaned. "Why won't you stop him?"

Kane gave him a wicked smile. "Not even Jamie is stupid enough to go after Angus. He's close to being feral."

Steven gasped. "And you let my granddaughter go with him?"

"Tell him," Erin rasped.

"Amie is the safest person in the world with him. She is the only one who can calm him before he loses it altogether."

Steven paled, nodded, and walked to Jarrod's side. "Can I have my daughter now, please?"

Kane shook his head. "Swap them around, Jarrod. Take your mate home, and I'll sort out her mother."

"Thanks. I'll ring tomorrow afternoon for an update." Jarrod gave Erin's mother to Steven, and Kane helped him with Erin. Jarrod went to his truck and gently placed Erin inside, strapping the seatbelt around her. Getting in the driver's side, he drove home, hoping everything worked out.

Chapter 4

Her mother was slowly getting better. In a week, a lot had happened. Erin now lived with Jarrod. Amie lived with Angus…well, ninety-five percent of the time. Amie wasn't happy about some of the new rules, especially being told she couldn't go out by herself, or without some protection.

Erin loved her new town and her new job at the fertility clinic. Kane had gotten her the job, and since werewolves already worked there she was safe. One of the things Erin loved most was that she didn't have to hide her gift, and she got to be herself. She now had loads of friends. She'd never really had a bunch of friends before because she couldn't risk her secrets being revealed. Not to mention that her family moved so often they always left before Erin could get close to anyone.

She couldn't get enough of Jarrod. Leaning over to him, she brushed her lips over his. Her hands glided down to explore his tight, hard body. Climbing up him, she straddled his waist and ran her fingers over him. Leaning down, she licked and sucked on his chest, slowing moving to her desired location.

He groaned and his eyes snapped opened. "Oh,

sweetheart, you're torturing me."

She grinned up at him as she reached his ridged erection. Her lips brushed over the tip before she took what she could into her mouth. Her hand came up and pumped what wouldn't fit.

Loud moans and grunts escaped his lips. Jarrod stilled as she picked up her pace, and she felt his cock stiffen even more as he growled. He flipped her over so she was on all fours and let out a loud howl that sent thrilling shivers coursing through her body. His fingers probed her wet pussy, sinking in and out. He nipped his way up her body before lining his dick up and slamming home

She screamed as her walls squeezed around him and the blaze inside her built. Bracing herself, she reveled in his quick, hard thrusts. Erin had never felt anything so good or so animalistic. She thrust back against him as he moved out, only to ram back in. Erin didn't realize she had such a naughty streak.

Her tits bounced, and she didn't know how much more of his onslaught she could take. The inferno inside her was about to explode. His teeth sunk into her shoulder and his hand came around and strummed at her clit. She fell apart, screaming her release. She could feel her walls hold his cock tight as it swelled and she quivered around him. Jarrod moaned against her shoulder and pumped a couple more times before she felt his warmth spread into her.

Spent, she collapsed on the bed and he followed, rolling them to the side. She sighed as he licked her shoulder and his arms came around her.

"I love you, Erin, and I can't wait to spend the rest of my life falling more in love with you every day. The more time I spend with you, the more I know how lucky I am."

Smiling, she snuggled into him. "I'm the lucky one. I'm so glad I forgot my gloves the night of Kane's party and I got to meet you. You helped me have a life, home, and friends. Thank you."

He kissed her shoulder. "No, thank you. You saved my soul, and I'm forever grateful. Thanks for saving this weary soldier and bringing life to me again."

Erin sighed, content, happy, and ready for the future.

About Hazel Gower

I'm a mother of four terrors between the ages of two and seven, and it's the best job in the world, well, other than being a writer.

I started writing down my story ideas in high school, and never really stopped. Writing, I have to say, is my salvation. After I've cleaned up and gotten all the kids in bed, I sit at my computer—or sometimes a notebook with a pencil—and relax, write, and escape.

I love to hear from any of my readers, so feel free to send me an email and 'like' me on Facebook.

Hazel's Website:

www.hazelgower.com

Reader eMail:

hazel.gower@yahoo.com.au

About the Armageddon Mates Series

Book 1: *Kane's Mate*

Now Available

Book 2: *Rane's Mate*

Now Available

Book 3: *Ava's Mate*

Coming Soon

CPSIA information can be obtained at www.ICGtesting.com
Printed in the USA
BVOW02s1708230813

329256BV00001B/4/P